The Cat Who Ate the End of the World

Copyright © 2025 by Kysa Steele

All rights reserved.

No part of this book may be reproduced in any form or by any electronic or mechanical means, including information storage and retrieval systems, without written permission from the author, except for the use of brief quotations in a book review.

This is a work of fiction. Names, characters, places, and incidents are either the product of the author's imagination or are used fictitiously. Any resemblance to actual persons, living or dead, or locales is entirely coincidental.

Kysa Steele

1st edition: 2026
ISBN: 978-1-971434-02-5 Paperback
ISBN: 978-1-971434-03-2 Hardback

Contents

1. The Consumption — 1
2. Bureaucratic Indigestion — 9
3. The Committee for the Prevention of Apocalyptic Inconvenience — 27
4. The Vote — 37
5. The Department of Increasingly Frantic Solutions — 47
6. The International Conference — 61
7. The Ask — 75
8. The Great Regurgitation Protocol — 91
9. The New Department of Mostly Satisfactory Endings — 109

Character List — 129
About the Author — 135
Also by Kysa Steele — 137

1
THE CONSUMPTION

"It has been said that cats are mysterious creatures. This is only true if you consider an open can of tuna mysterious, which most cats do not."

Mungus was a cat of simple philosophy. If it fit in his mouth, it was probably food. If it didn't fit in his mouth, it might still be food if approached from the right angle, with sufficient determination, and possibly the assistance of gravity.

This approach to life had served him well for all of his seven years, though it had led to some regrettable incidents involving houseplants, shoelaces, and on one memorable occasion, a small postal worker who had inexplicably decided to nap in the front garden.

Claire Pemberton had adopted Mungus three years ago, primarily because he was the only cat in the shelter who didn't flee when she mentioned her field of study. Most animals seemed to possess an instinctive understanding that Applied Apocalyptics was not a career path that attracted stable personalities. Mungus, however, had simply looked at her with the measured attention of someone evaluating a potential food service provider.

Food lady. Smells like books and worry. Good enough.

To Mungus, their relationship was a simple transaction of provisions. For Claire, it had evolved into a crucial partnership for her academic survival. She provided food, shelter, and a steady supply of interesting objects to investigate. He provided companionship, a warm presence during late-night thesis writing sessions, and an uncanny ability to knock expensive takeaway containers off the table at precisely the moment when Claire could least afford to reorder.

"You realize," Claire said, addressing Mungus as he began his evening patrol, "that my entire academic career is sitting on that table, weighed down by objects that Professor Blackwood says could theoretically end civilization?"

She ran a hand through her hair, feeling three years' work pressing down on her—and her mother's voice asking when she'd get a 'real job', and the department's skepticism about whether anyone should be studying apocalypses that had already happened. It was more than just a degree; it was a desperate need to prove that past civilizations hadn't just died, they had tried to warn those who came after. If she could prove that, maybe this time someone would listen. The Seal of Final Things was supposed to prove them all wrong. If she could decode its warning systems, she might finally validate her field, show that studying how civilizations destroy themselves wasn't just academic navel-gazing but practical survival knowledge.

Of course, convincing her mother that Applied

Apocalyptics was practical would require a miracle. Or possibly an actual apocalypse.

From Mungus's perspective, this was just another round of mouth-sounds that didn't involve food.

Food lady making noise. Not about dinner. Continue patrol.

The flat reflected both Claire's academic focus and her complete inability to organize anything that wasn't directly related to cosmic catastrophe. Books with apocalyptic titles were stacked everywhere, held down by what looked like rocks but were actually artifacts from civilizations that had successfully ended their own worlds. Several of these "paperweights" retained enough residual cosmic significance to make any practicing mystic break out in nervous sweats—though to Mungus, they were simply objects that sometimes smelled interesting and occasionally provided warm spots for napping.

Tonight was different, though. The paperweight holding down Claire's thesis wasn't just any old artifact—it was the Seal of Final Things, and Claire had spent the last month convinced it might actually save her academic career.

"This is it, Mungus," she had told him that morning, carefully placing the Seal next to her dinner plate where it could hold down Chapter Three. "Professor Blackwood says if I can decode the warning systems on this thing, I might actually graduate before my student loans achieve sentience."

The Seal had arrived at the University via the usual channels—someone's grandmother's attic—and Professor Blackwood had declared it "moderately ominous but probably dormant." He hadn't mentioned that "dormant" cosmic artifacts had a tendency to respond to proximity to other cosmic forces, of which Claire's flat now contained an impressive and entirely accidental collection.

Claire's thesis argued that civilizations that destroyed themselves had been thoughtful about leaving warnings for future civilizations. The problem was that future civilizations used these warnings as decorative objects. The Seal was supposed to be her proof, a perfect example of apocalyptic foresight being reduced to paperweight duty.

Her preliminary analysis suggested the Seal contained what appeared to be some kind of instruction manual, written in symbols that were almost familiar, like a language she had once dreamed of. Three more months of work, maybe four, and she'd have enough for her final chapter. Then she could stop eating ramen noodles for dinner and start proving that her unconventional field had merit.

"Just don't eat this one, okay?" Claire had warned Mungus that morning. "I know you think everything that glows is probably food, but this might actually be important."

In Mungus's experience, everything might potentially be food.

Will investigate later when food lady not watching.

Now, as Claire worked in the living room, wrestling with academic formatting requirements that seemed designed to test one's commitment to scholarship through sheer tedium, Mungus moved his investigation to the kitchen table.

The table presented several interesting opportunities from his perspective. Claire's dinner sat cooling in its container, chopsticks balanced precariously on the edge. The smell reached his nose as a mixture of soy sauce and mild disappointment—Tuesday Special from the place that delivered but never quite lived up to its name.

More intriguingly, there was something else. Something that smelled distinctly of fish.

The object sat next to Claire's plate, about the size of a cricket ball. It appeared to be made of some kind of clear material that caught the kitchen light. Inside, miniature storms swirled through crystalline depths, occasionally illuminated by flashes of lightning that existed in dimensions slightly adjacent to the kitchen.

Shiny thing. Fish smell. Want.

To any cosmic theorist, the Seal would have radiated enough warning signals to evacuate a small city. To Mungus, it was simply something shiny that smelled appealingly of fish—the Seal's fishy aroma being the result of its last activation, a millennia ago, when it had been used to prevent the collapse of an empire whose primary export had been inter-dimensional seafood. This detail would have fascinated Claire's academic advisors, but was entirely irrelevant to Mungus's decision-making process.

In Mungus's experience, things that glowed usually didn't fight back, and things that smelled like fish were generally worth investigating. The combination was promising.

Glows. Good smell. No angry sounds. Safe.

The Seal of Final Things, being an inanimate object containing the compressed essence of several cosmic endings, had no capacity for the defensive behaviors Mungus had learned to associate with inadvisable food choices. It couldn't hiss, attempt to flee, or manifest protective spells.

From the living room came the sound of rapid typing interspersed with small frustrated noises. In Mungus's experience, this meant at least twenty minutes of uninterrupted human distraction.

Coast clear. Time for investigation.

He approached the Seal with the focused determination that had once enabled him to consume an entire rotisserie chicken while his previous family dealt with a small kitchen fire. The technique was refined through years of practice: quick assessment, strategic positioning, decisive action.

The object crunched pleasantly between his teeth, rather like the expensive treats Claire occasionally purchased when her guilt about leaving him alone during long library sessions reached critical levels.

Crunchy. Good texture. Tastes like... chicken? With weird aftertaste.

The 'weird aftertaste' was actually the essence of existential dread mixed with oregano—a combination that had driven at least three cosmic theorists to early retirement. Mungus made a mental note about management's questionable seasoning choices.

The artifact settled in his stomach with a warm sensation that felt remarkably like the satisfaction of a substantial meal.

Good food. Will complain about strange taste later. Maybe food lady fix.

From the living room came the sound of Claire saving her work and stretching in her chair. In approximately ninety seconds, she would come to check on her cooling dinner and discover that her thesis paperweight had mysteriously vanished. This would eventually trigger a sequence of events requiring the formation of several new government departments, but such implications were far beyond the scope of Mungus's current concerns.

Nap time. Find warm spot.

He padded to his favorite cardboard box—an Amazon container that had once held Claire's textbooks on theoretical catastrophe management and now served as his primary headquarters for observing household activities while maintaining plausible deniability.

As he settled into the perfectly cat-sized depression he had created over months of dedicated napping, the odd aftertaste seemed to echo with distant voices discussing things he couldn't quite grasp. In Mungus's experience, strange dreams were best ignored in favor of more practical concerns.

Weird dreams coming. Think about tuna instead.

Tomorrow, he decided, he would definitely need to have a conversation with management about proper seasoning. If shiny objects were going to taste like chicken, they should at least taste like good chicken, preferably with a tuna marinade.

"Mungus?" Claire's voice drifted from the kitchen, carrying a note of confusion that would soon escalate into academic panic. "Where's my paperweight? Mungus? MUNGUS!"

But Mungus was already settling into sleep, his consciousness drifting toward dreams of vast oceans filled with properly seasoned fish. He had just consumed Claire's best hope for academic success along with a load-bearing wall in the architecture of reality itself.

Meanwhile, the space where the Seal of Final Things

had been sitting began to emit a small, polite humming sound, as if reality was clearing its throat to mention that something rather important had gone missing. The sound was too subtle for human ears but registered on dozens of pieces of monitoring equipment scattered across London, all of which began updating their cosmic threat assessments from "moderate concern" to "someone should probably look into this."

Elsewhere in the city, a cosmic alarm clock that had been faithfully counting down to the end of the world for the past four millennia checked its settings, found itself suddenly without a schedule to follow, and began emitting a low, confused hum that began to disturb the sleep of three nearby clairvoyants and one surprisingly sensitive pigeon.

2
Bureaucratic Indigestion

"The trouble with eating something that wasn't meant to be eaten is that it tends to disagree with you. The trouble with eating the cosmic lynchpin of reality is that reality tends to disagree with everyone else."

In a windowless monitoring station beneath Whitehall, Technician Grade 2, David Dawson, sipped his lukewarm tea and watched the screens. The North London Cosmic Array, usually a sea of placid green data points, was screaming in twelve-dimensional color. The primary emission signature wasn't a stellar event, a temporal distortion, or a standard dimensional breach. According to the diagnostic algorithm, whose frantic pop-up windows David kept dismissing, the signature was organic, feline, and currently... purring.

He picked up the secure phone with the calm professionalism of a man paid not to panic.

"Sir," he said to the department head, "you need to see this. I think we have an unscheduled cat."

Wednesday morning arrived in Claire's flat with a cheerful insistence that suggested the universe was either completely unaware that one of its fundamental support structures had been digested, or was putting on a brave face while quietly panicking behind the scenes. The sun rose precisely on schedule, birds sang their dawn chorus with suspicious regularity, and somewhere in North London, a cosmic alarm clock continued to hum in confusion.

Claire woke up to find Mungus sitting on her chest, staring at her with the intense focus that usually meant either he was hungry or something required immediate attention. Given that her alarm clock was displaying what appeared to be hieroglyphics instead of numbers, she suspected it might be both.

Food lady awake. Strange taste still in mouth. Want breakfast.

"Good morning to you too," she mumbled, gently moving him aside so she could sit up. "Did you sleep well, or did you spend all night digesting cosmic forces beyond mortal comprehension?"

His response—a purr that seemed to have gained several new harmonics overnight—caused her bedside lamp to flicker briefly through colors that didn't technically exist in the visible spectrum.

Purr feels different. More vibrations. Nice.

"Right," Claire said, noting that her spider plant, which had been a cheerful green companion for three years, was now glowing softly and appeared to be trying to communicate through interpretive leaf-rustling. "I think we need to have a serious conversation about your dietary choices."

She had always talked to him during their morning routine, but today felt different. Today, she found herself studying his face with the desperate attention of someone realizing they might lose something precious and irreplaceable.

"You know," she said, scratching behind his ears while he purred his strangely enhanced purr, "I've gotten rather used to having you around. I realize that makes me the stereotype of the lonely graduate student with a cat, but you're excellent company for someone whose social life consists mainly of arguing with dusty books and attending committee meetings about the end of the world."

Good scratches. Food lady making worried sounds again.

When he leaned into her hand, his shift in position caused the wallpaper behind her bed to begin displaying aurora effects. Claire felt her familiar academic panic rising—research was becoming personal in ways she hadn't anticipated.

"Whatever's happening to you," she said quietly, "we'll figure it out. I'm not losing you to some cosmic indigestion, okay? I've read enough apocalyptic literature to know that these things usually have solutions, even if they're ridiculous ones."

Food lady upset. Should investigate kitchen for breakfast.

As Claire made her way to the kitchen, she couldn't shake the growing fear that this might be the kind of problem that required solutions she wasn't prepared to implement. What if helping Mungus meant letting the government take him away? What if cosmic significance was incompatible with being a house cat?

The kitchen presented an even more concerning tableau than her bedroom. Claire's dinner plate from the previous evening still sat on the table, but where the Seal of Final Things had once provided convenient paperweight services, there was now only a faint scorch mark in the shape of something that might have been a symbol.

Empty food bowl. This problem.

More immediately problematic was her spider plant, which had achieved what any cosmic theorist would recognize as full enlightenment and was glowing with such intensity that she could read her thesis notes by its light. As Claire watched, the plant's leaves began trembling with profound philosophical realization, then suddenly went limp with the quiet dignity of something that had seen too much truth too quickly.

"Well," Claire said to Mungus, who was investigating his food bowl with disappointed attention, "that's not ominous at all."

Food bowl empty. Plant acting strange. Food lady nervous. All problems.

Seven years in Applied Apocalyptics had taught Claire to treat impossible situations with methodical calm. Step one: assess the situation. Step two: consult the literature. Step three: file the appropriate paperwork. Step four: panic quietly while maintaining professional composure.

"Mungus," she said, opening her laptop and pulling up the University's emergency protocols, "I need you to stay right there while I figure out who to call about cosmic pet emergencies. Can you do that for me?"

Food lady making mouth sounds. Not about food. Continue morning patrol.

His morning grooming session immediately caused the coffee machine to start brewing beverages that smelled like they came from a universe where coffee had evolved differently. The resulting purr sent harmonic vibrations through the flat that made Claire's thesis notes rearrange themselves into more aesthetically pleasing configurations.

Good grooming. Fur properly arranged. Strange coffee smell interesting.

Claire stared at the University's online forms portal, wondering how she was going to explain that she'd lost a potentially world-ending artifact to feline dietary adventurism. Form PET-7/MISC-COSMIC (Notification of Displaced Artifacts with Potential for Public Inconvenience) was a masterpiece of bureaucratic complexity designed by people who believed dangerous objects should be too intimidated by paperwork to go missing.

The form's requirement to report an object's last known emotional state had been added after the infamous incident with the Depressed Dagger of Despair, which had gone missing for three weeks and was eventually found hiding in a supply closet, crying softly to itself.

She was halfway through the section on "Possible Alternative Dimensions Where Object Might Currently Reside" when her doorbell rang with unusual urgency—the staccato insistence of someone pressing the button repeatedly and with no intention of stopping until acknowledged.

Loud noise at door. Strangers coming. Alert.

Professor Blackwood stood on her doorstep, looking like

a man who had received urgent calls from instruments that shouldn't exist. He was carrying a briefcase that appeared to be humming softly and vibrating with barely contained technological panic.

"Claire," he said, without preamble, "please tell me you haven't lost the Seal of Final Things."

"I was just filling out Form PET-7," Claire replied, which conveyed the essential information while buying her a few seconds to process the implications of her advisor appearing with emergency supernatural detection equipment.

Professor Blackwood closed his eyes and appeared to be counting to ten in several different ancient languages.

"May I come in? And where is your cat?"

"He's in the kitchen, having an existential crisis with my coffee machine," Claire said, stepping aside. "Professor, is Mungus in danger? Because I need to know that before we start talking about the artifact or the paperwork. Is my cat going to be okay?"

The direct question surprised Professor Blackwood, who paused. When he met her eyes, the academic detachment had slipped.

"That," he said, "is actually the most important question you could ask right now. The honest answer is that I don't know. We're in uncharted territory here, Claire. But I can tell you that your cat is almost certainly not in immediate physical danger—cosmic artifacts tend to be quite considerate about their hosts."

"Hosts?" Claire's voice cracked slightly on the word.

"Poor choice of terminology," Professor Blackwood held up a hand. "I meant... well, we'll figure out what I meant once I can get some proper readings."

New person smells like chalk and old books. Investigating.

Mungus chose that moment to make his appearance, padding into the hallway with casual confidence. He paused to rub against Professor Blackwood's legs in greeting—a gesture that caused the Professor's briefcase to begin chiming like a small church bell having a nervous breakdown.

"That," said Professor Blackwood, staring down at Mungus with the expression of someone solving an unpleasant equation, "is definitely not a normal cat anymore."

Legs smell interesting. Good for rubbing.

Claire felt her heart sink. "What do you mean, not normal? He's still Mungus. He still likes having his chin scratched and he still knocks things off tables for no reason. He's just... enhanced."

Professor Blackwood set his briefcase down to reveal instruments that looked like they had been designed by someone who understood both advanced physics and traditional witchcraft. Several were pointing directly at Mungus and emitting urgent beeping sounds.

"According to my measurements," Professor Blackwood continued, consulting a device that resembled a cross between a Geiger counter and a crystal ball, "your cat is currently registering cosmic significance levels that are technically off the scale. The scale, I should mention, was designed to measure the apocalyptic potential of small countries."

Shoes smell like interesting dust. Worth investigating.

Mungus was being subjected to scientific analysis while

investigating Professor Blackwood's shoes with the thoroughness of a health inspector.

"But he's still himself," Claire said, crouching down to scratch Mungus behind the ears. His purr immediately caused the hallway light fixtures to emit what appeared to be tiny fireworks. "Look, he's happy. He's not in pain or distressed or anything. Can't we just monitor the situation? Keep him comfortable while we figure out what to do?"

Good scratches. Pretty lights. Food lady less worried now.

"Claire," Professor Blackwood said, "I understand your attachment to your pet. But we may be looking at a situation where the cat's comfort and the continued existence of reality are in conflict."

Before Claire could respond to this unwelcome possibility, Mungus developed what felt like a hairball.

Throat feels scratchy. Need to cough.

His usual direct approach to hairball management resulted in a coughing sound accompanied by a small shower of sparks and the brief manifestation of a very polite demon.

The demon was about the size of a house cat, with the mismatched features of a creature designed by a committee that couldn't agree on whether it should be intimidating or adorable. Its small horns were filed for safety, it had decorative wings, and an expression of profound embarrassment.

"Oh, dear," it said, in a voice like a nervous librarian, "I do apologize for the inconvenience. I seem to have been inadvertently summoned. This is most irregular."

Small creature appeared. Smells like old paper and sadness. Not threatening.

Claire stared at the demon, then at Mungus, then at Professor Blackwood.

Professor Blackwood was staring at Harold with the expression of someone whose entire academic career had just been validated in the most inconvenient way possible. His hands trembled slightly as he set down his instruments, his composure—usually as solid as a tenured professorship—visibly cracking.

"It's real," he said, his voice carrying the wonder of a man who'd spent decades studying theory. "After thirty years of studying theoretical manifestations, I'm looking at an actual demon. A polite one, no less." He laughed, a bit shakily. "All those papers I've written, all the academic debates about classification and materialization patterns, and none of it prepared me for... for biscuits and apologies."

"Professor?" Claire asked, concerned by the unusual display of emotion.

"I'm fine," he said, still staring at Harold with wonder. "It's just rather different when theory becomes practice. Rather more real than I'd imagined." He paused. "Would anyone like some tea? Because I genuinely think we're going to need it, and I need a moment to process that demons are apparently real and extremely polite."

The demon—Harold—perked up considerably. "Oh, that would be lovely, thank you. I don't suppose you have any biscuits? Summoning always makes me rather peckish."

New creature likes food sounds. Possibly useful.

Twenty minutes later, just as Claire was serving tea to a demon while trying not to cry about the possibility of losing her cat to cosmic forces, there was another knock at the door.

Agent Martinez from the Ministry of Defence: Special Projects and Irregular Situations Branch stood on the doorstep with the air of someone who had been expecting this call but wasn't particularly happy about being right. She was a woman in her forties with the practical demeanor of someone whose job involved preparing for impossible situations, and she carried a briefcase significantly larger than Professor Blackwood's that made considerably more ominous noises.

"Dr. Pemberton?" she said, consulting a self-updating clipboard. "I'm Agent Martinez. I understand you may have a situation involving an unauthorized cosmic entity?"

The phrase "unauthorized cosmic entity" sent a chill through Claire.

"That depends," Claire replied, her protective instincts flaring immediately, "on whether you're referring to my cat, because if you are, I need you to understand that he's not an 'entity'—he's a living creature who I care about very much. And if you're here to treat him like a problem to be solved rather than—"

"Dr. Pemberton," Agent Martinez interrupted, "I appreciate your emotional attachment to the animal, but we need to establish the facts of the situation before we can determine appropriate containment protocols. The entity—"

"His name is Mungus," Claire said, stepping partially into the doorway in a way that was probably futile but felt necessary. "And he's not getting 'contained' anywhere without me."

Agent Martinez's expression didn't change. "Dr. Pemberton, I realize this is distressing, but temporal anomalies of this magnitude require immediate assessment and potential isolation. Whether the variable appears in feline form is irrelevant to—"

"The variable?" Claire's voice rose. "You're talking about my cat like he's a piece of equipment. He has feelings, he has preferences, he—"

"Can generate reality distortions powerful enough to affect several city blocks," Agent Martinez checked her clipboard. "Which is why the Ministry needs to assess whether the entity can be safely maintained in a civilian environment or whether transfer to a secure facility is necessary."

Claire felt her heart hammering. This was exactly what she'd feared—bureaucrats showing up to turn Mungus into a file number.

"You're not taking him," she said, hearing the tremor in her voice but pushing through it. "I don't care what protocols you have or what forms need to be filled out. Mungus stays with me, or you're going to have to explain to your supervisors why you couldn't handle one graduate student without creating an even bigger problem than a cosmic cat."

For the first time, Agent Martinez's professional mask cracked slightly. Her eyes narrowed as she reassessed Claire.

"Dr. Pemberton, are you threatening a Ministry official?"

"I'm establishing boundaries," Claire said, surprised by her own boldness. "And making it clear that any solution that doesn't include Mungus's well-being and our staying together is not a solution I'm going to cooperate with. You can file that in whatever form requires the most paperwork."

Then, unexpectedly, Agent Martinez's expression softened—just slightly, but noticeably.

"May I come in?" she asked, and her tone had shifted.

The bureaucratic edge was gone. "I think we may have gotten off on the wrong foot. Let me start over."

She stepped inside, and when she spoke again, her voice carried genuine warmth.

"Dr. Pemberton, I apologize. That was... unnecessarily clinical. I've been doing this job for fifteen years, and sometimes I forget that 'unauthorized cosmic entity' means someone's beloved pet." She paused. "I want to be clear about something from the start. Our primary goal is the safety and well-being of all parties involved, including your cat. We're not here to separate you from your pet—we're here to make sure everyone survives this situation intact."

Claire felt some of the tension leave her shoulders, though she remained wary. "That's what I needed to hear. But I meant what I said. Mungus and I are a package deal."

"Understood," Agent Martinez said, and this time she seemed to mean it. "Now, everything counts as something—the question is whether it counts as something we can file paperwork about or something that requires emergency protocols."

She paused in the hallway, consulted an instrument that looked like a mobile phone crossed with a dowsing rod, and nodded with satisfaction.

"Definitely emergency protocols," she said. "Is the cat available for consultation?"

New person smell. Official smells. Worth investigating.

Mungus, as if summoned by the mention of his name, appeared from the living room. He had apparently made friends with the demon, who was now perched on his back like a small, horned rider.

Small creature comfortable. Good weight for carrying.

"Harold," the demon said by way of introduction, waving cheerfully at Agent Martinez. "I'm a Class C Manifestation of Mild Inconvenience. Terribly sorry about the unscheduled appearance."

Harold shifted slightly on Mungus's back, looking between Claire and Agent Martinez with understanding.

"If I may," Harold said quietly, "I was originally summoned during a filing error at the Ministry of Minor Inconveniences. Spent three decades causing paperwork to disappear just when people needed it most. I know what it's like when bureaucracy separates beings who belong together." He looked directly at Claire. "We won't let that happen to you and Mungus."

Small creature makes good sounds for food lady. Good creature.

Claire felt tears of relief gathering. "Thank you, Harold. That means everything."

Agent Martinez made notes on her clipboard—a standard-issue Adaptive Documentation Device that could generate appropriate forms for any situation, no matter how unprecedented.

"No problem, Harold. We'll get you sorted out with the proper forms. Now, about the cat..."

Agent Martinez crouched down to Mungus's level and regarded him with the professional interest of someone who had extensive experience with supernatural pet care—but this time, her expression held something warmer than clinical assessment.

New person wants attention. Will provide purr.

His purr created an immediate and dramatic effect. Agent Martinez's hair stood on end, her clipboard began displaying stock market information from several different dimensions, and somewhere in the distance, a car alarm went off for no apparent reason.

"Right," she said, standing up and smoothing down her hair with practiced efficiency. "I think we can officially classify this as a Feline-Related Cosmic Event, Class A-7. These events involve cats that have consumed reality-affecting substances and are classified as 'dangerous but probably manageable with adequate paperwork.'"

Claire felt a surge of hope. "Manageable sounds good. Manageable sounds like Mungus gets to stay with me."

"That's certainly our preferred outcome," Agent Martinez said. "But I'll need to make some calls to get the proper support team assembled."

She selected a device that resembled a telephone crossed with a small telescope and began dialing a number with more digits than should be necessary.

"Emergency Operations?" she said into the device. "Martinez here. We have a confirmed FRCE-A7 in North London. Request immediate deployment of Forms Package Delta-7 and a pot of tea. Strong tea."

She listened for a moment, made notes that seemed to write themselves, and nodded.

"Understood. Yes, I know it's Wednesday. No, I don't think that makes it any less urgent. Because," she added, glancing at Mungus, who was now attempting to groom Harold the demon, "the cat appears to have eaten something that was keeping reality properly organized, and reality is starting to notice."

Small creature needs grooming. Important task.

His grooming session caused the kitchen fluorescent lights to briefly display aurora effects, while Harold made small contented noises that sounded suspiciously like demonic purring.

Agent Martinez hung up and turned to face the assembled group with the air of someone delivering news that would require additional paperwork.

"The good news," she said, "is that we have protocols for this sort of thing. The bad news is that the protocols were written by a committee that may have been slightly insane. The worse news is that we're going to need to fill out forms that haven't been invented yet."

Claire looked around her kitchen, which now contained a professor, a government agent, a demon having tea, and a cat who was apparently responsible for cosmic instability but still wanted his breakfast.

"I should probably mention,"—Claire's voice had given out somewhere around the sentient refrigerator—"that I still haven't finished Form PET-7."

Agent Martinez offered a professionally sympathetic smile, one she had clearly used in similar situations before.

"Don't worry," she said. "After today, Form PET-7 is going to be the least of your problems. Now, shall we discuss temporary relocation procedures, or would you prefer to wait until something more dramatic happens?"

"Temporary relocation?" Claire's voice sharpened with alarm, her earlier wariness returning. "You mean taking Mungus somewhere? Because I'm not letting him out of my sight until I know he's going to be okay."

"Dr. Pemberton," Agent Martinez said, and there was

real understanding in her voice now, "the relocation would be for all of you—you, the cat, Harold, and Professor Blackwood. We have secure facilities that are designed to handle cosmic instability while we work on solutions. You wouldn't be separated from your cat. I promise you that."

Small creature making approval sounds. Good.

Harold shifted slightly on Mungus's back, making a small approving sound. "Quite right," he murmured softly. "Proper partnerships shouldn't be disrupted by paperwork."

Grooming finished. Time for nap.

When Mungus finished grooming Harold and settled down for a proper nap, his contented purring filled the kitchen with harmonic resonances that caused the refrigerator to briefly achieve sentience, consider the implications of its existence, and return to its normal state of keeping things cold.

"I think," said Professor Blackwood, watching the refrigerator with fascination, "we should definitely accept the relocation offer."

Agent Martinez nodded and began unpacking emergency forms from her briefcase. "Standard procedure for Class A-7 events. We'll need to move everyone to a secure facility while we figure out how to handle a cat who has accidentally become a cosmic phenomenon without compromising his essential catness."

"His essential catness?" Claire asked.

"It's a technical term," Agent Martinez didn't smile. "One of our primary concerns in these situations is making sure that cosmic enhancement doesn't interfere with the entity's fundamental nature. In this case, we want to make sure your cat remains, essentially, a cat who happens to have cosmic significance, rather than becoming a cosmic force that used to be a cat."

This distinction was important—it determined whether Mungus would retain his personality and attachment to her, or transform into something beyond mortal comprehension. Claire found it oddly comforting that the government had policies about preserving the personality traits of cosmically significant pets.

"What about Harold?" Claire asked, gesturing to the demon, who was now curled up on Mungus's back like a small, horned cushion.

"Harold comes too," Martinez was already making notes. "Unauthorized summonings require proper documentation, and we can't document him if he's not available for processing."

Harold perked up from his position on Mungus's back. "Oh, I do so love forms," he said cheerfully. "They make everything so wonderfully official."

Small creature happy about paper things. Strange but harmless.

Claire looked around her kitchen one more time, taking in the scorch mark where her paperweight had been, the glowing wallpaper, the satisfied cat with his demon passenger, and the government agent who—after a rocky start—seemed genuinely committed to keeping them all together.

"Alright," she said. "Let's go fill out some forms and figure out how to save the world without losing my cat. But I'm bringing his favorite cardboard box, and if anyone tries to separate us, I'm going to become a much bigger problem than cosmic instability."

Cardboard box coming. Important.

Agent Martinez smiled—a real smile this time, not the professional mask from earlier. "Dr. Pemberton, I think you're going to fit in just fine with our crisis management team."

3
THE COMMITTEE FOR THE PREVENTION OF APOCALYPTIC INCONVENIENCE

"Committees are proof that humans can take any problem, no matter how urgent, and turn it into a reason to have tea and biscuits. They are also proof that the person with the most paperwork usually wins."

The Secure Facility turned out to be a converted office building in South London that was a study in beige, as if designed by someone who believed it was the most calming color in the universe. The building had the institutional charm of a place that had been hastily repurposed for handling situations too unusual for normal government departments but not quite unusual enough to warrant their own dedicated buildings.

Moving box smells like food lady worry. Don't like moving box.

Claire found herself clutching Mungus's carrier as they were led through corridors lined with motivational posters featuring cats hanging from tree branches. The irony was not lost on her—here she was, walking through a government facility with a cosmically significant cat, past posters that probably predated anyone's awareness that cats could achieve cosmic significance.

"I don't like this," she whispered to Mungus through the carrier's mesh window. "Government buildings make me nervous, and that's before you factor in cosmic cat emergencies. These places always smell like disinfectant and broken dreams."

Food lady making worried sounds. Building smells like chemicals and fear-sweat.

His responding purr caused the nearest motivational poster to briefly display ancient prophecies in cuneiform script before reverting to its original message about teamwork. The transformation was accompanied by a soft golden glow that made the beige corridor momentarily beautiful.

"At least you're adapting better than I am," Claire said with a weak smile, watching him settle more comfortably in his carrier. She had packed his favorite blanket—a threadbare thing that had once been blue but was now the color of comfort and cat hair—and seeing him burrow into it made her feel slightly less like she was delivering him to some cosmic fate beyond her control.

Good blanket. Smells like home and food lady.

Harold the demon had taken to institutional life with alarming enthusiasm that suggested he had finally found his true calling. Within twenty minutes of their arrival, he had appointed himself unofficial filing assistant and was reorganizing emergency paperwork with the dedication of someone who had discovered that bureaucracy was actually a form of performance art.

"This is wonderful," Harold announced, clutching a stack of forms to his small chest with reverence other creatures might reserve for sacred texts. "Everything is so properly categorized! Look, they have subsections for 'Supernatural Pet Emergencies' and 'Cosmic Dietary Incidents'—someone actually anticipated this situation!"

Harold had set up a small workstation in the corner, complete with a typewriter that appeared to be from the 1940s but was somehow connected to a computer system that definitely wasn't. The clicking of his typing had developed a rhythmic quality that seemed to help organize the chaos around them.

Small creature makes nice clicking sounds. Soothing.

In a situation where everything felt surreal and potentially dangerous, Claire found herself oddly grateful for Harold's presence. There was something comforting about having someone around who was genuinely excited about the paperwork.

The Emergency Committee had assembled with remarkable speed. Claire found herself in Conference Room B with the assembled officials, one cat who was technically the subject of the entire proceeding, and Harold, who had appointed himself official note-taker and was typing with demonic enthusiasm.

New room. Many people. Some smell anxious. Some smell like old papers.

She released Mungus from his carrier, and he immediately began investigating the conference room with methodical attention. The transformation of ordinary sunlight into something resembling the northern lights accompanied his movement—Claire watched him pad through the colored light, his fur picking up hints of green and gold that shouldn't exist in a conference room in South London.

Pretty lights. Warm on fur. Good spot for later exploration.

To the committee members, he looked like himself but also like something more—an ordinary house cat who had accidentally become a small miracle.

"Before we begin," Claire said, standing up as the committee members arranged themselves around the table, "I need to make something absolutely clear."

Food lady using loud voice. Important sounds.

The room fell silent, faces turning toward Claire with expressions ranging from professional interest to barely concealed panic.

"You're talking about my cat," she continued, her voice steady, though her hands had gone cold. "Mungus isn't a problem to be solved or a weapon to be contained. He's my family. So before we start discussing protocols and procedures, I need someone to look me in the eye and promise that we're not going to hurt him."

Food lady making protective sounds. Good food lady.

Claire counted three heartbeats before Agent Martinez nodded with what appeared to be genuine warmth.

"Dr. Pemberton, I appreciate your directness," she said. "Let me be absolutely clear: our primary goal is the safety and well-being of all parties involved, including your cat.

We're here to find a solution that keeps everyone happy, healthy, and hopefully still existing in this dimension."

"Thank you," Claire said, feeling some of the tension leave her shoulders. "I just needed to hear that officially. And on the record."

Food lady sounds less worried now. Good.

A man Claire hadn't noticed before cleared his throat with a pointed aggression that suggested he was used to being the most important person in any room. He was thin, severe-looking, with the tight expression of someone who viewed kindness as a line item that could be eliminated from the budget. But unlike the bureaucrats Claire had encountered before—the ones who seemed to stumble into opposition through sheer institutional momentum—this man had the focused energy of someone who had prepared.

"Dr. Pemberton," he said, his voice sharp as scissors, "I'm Gerald Harwick, Assistant Deputy Under-Secretary for Fiscal Oversight and Resource Allocation." He opened a leather portfolio with deliberate care, revealing not just a tablet but organized folders, printed documents, and what was clearly a timeline. "I've taken the liberty of preparing a comprehensive analysis of this situation."

New person sounds hostile. Organized hostile. Don't like organized hostile.

Claire felt her protective instincts flare. Harwick had prepared. The folders, the timeline, the quotes from her university records—this wasn't institutional momentum. This was targeted. It made her nervous in a way simple hostility wouldn't have.

"Before we discuss the animal," Harwick continued, "I think we need to discuss Dr. Pemberton herself." He looked up, meeting her eyes with cold precision. "Specifically, whether she is the appropriate person to be involved in these proceedings at all."

No one moved. Even Harold's typing stopped.

"Excuse me?" Claire said.

"You are, by your own admission, emotionally compromised," Harwick said, consulting his notes. "You've already stated that the entity is 'family' to you. You've made demands of this committee before we've even begun deliberations. And according to your university records—" he produced a document Claire recognized—her own accommodation request from three years ago"—you have a documented history of anxiety that has required academic accommodations."

Food lady's heart beating faster. Hostile person attacking food lady now.

"That's—that's completely irrelevant," Claire stammered, caught off guard. "My mental health has nothing to do with—"

"It has everything to do with whether you can be trusted to make objective assessments about a potential threat to national security," Harwick said smoothly. "The entity has already demonstrated reality-warping capabilities. You've admitted you would prioritize its well-being over other considerations. How can this committee trust that you would report accurately if the situation deteriorated? How can we be certain you wouldn't conceal dangerous developments to protect your... pet?"

Claire opened her mouth to respond, but Harwick was already moving on, addressing the room.

"I want to be clear: I'm not suggesting Dr. Pemberton has

done anything wrong. I'm suggesting that her emotional involvement makes her unsuitable as a primary contact for an entity of this significance. We need objective handlers. Professionals who can make difficult decisions without personal attachment clouding their judgment."

Hostile person trying to separate me from food lady. Very bad. Very angry.

Mungus's tail began to twitch. The fluorescent lights flickered, and Harwick's tablet screen briefly displayed static before returning to normal.

"The entity's reaction to my statements," Harwick noted calmly, gesturing at the flickering lights, "only proves my point. It responds to Dr. Pemberton's emotional state. If she becomes distressed, it becomes unstable. This feedback loop is precisely what we cannot afford in a crisis management situation."

Dr. Wilhelmina Crumpet—a woman in her sixties who had achieved academic tenure by proving that impossible things were not only possible but statistically inevitable—adjusted her spectacles. "Mr. Harwick, the bond between the cat and Dr. Pemberton appears to be a stabilizing factor, not a destabilizing one."

"With respect, Dr. Crumpet, that's a hypothesis, not a proven fact," Harwick replied. "And even if true, it raises the question: are we comfortable making national security decisions based on the emotional stability of a graduate student?"

Old lady trying to help. Hostile person prepared for this.

He turned to the Deputy Minister for Reality Maintenance, a tired-looking man who had been quietly reviewing documents. "Minister Warren, I'd like to present Treasury's formal assessment."

The Deputy Minister nodded wearily. "Go ahead, Mr. Harwick."

Harwick stood, distributing folders to each committee member with the efficiency of someone who had done this many times before. Claire watched helplessly as her fate—and Mungus's—was literally handed around the table in beige manila folders.

"Option One: Surgical extraction. Our veterinary consultants have advised against this due to temporal complications. I concur that this option is not viable at present."

Surgery bad word. But hostile person agreeing surgery bad. Confusing.

"Option Two: Passive observation while the artifact dissolves naturally. Timeline unknown, ranging from days to millennia. During this period, reality disturbances would continue and likely escalate. Unacceptable from a public safety standpoint."

"Option Three: The proposal Agent Martinez has outlined. Creation of a new ministry, permanent government support, Dr. Pemberton appointed as primary caretaker. Estimated annual cost: two million pounds, indefinitely. No clear endpoint. No accountability metrics. No contingency if the situation worsens."

He paused, letting the numbers sink in.

"I would like to propose Option Four."

New option. Don't like how hostile person says 'option four.'

Claire's fingers tightened on the arm of her chair. Agent Martinez caught her eye with a look that seemed to say *wait*.

"Temporary secure housing," Harwick said, "in a facility designed for cosmic anomaly containment. The entity would be comfortable, well-cared for, and monitored by trained professionals. Dr. Pemberton would have supervised visitation rights while we gather more data. Once we fully understand the situation, we can make a permanent decision based on evidence rather than emotion."

"You're talking about taking my cat," Claire said, her voice breaking.

"I'm talking about a reasonable precautionary measure," Harwick replied. "The entity has opened portals, altered documents, affected weather patterns, and caused fish to rain on South London. These are not the actions of a normal pet. The question isn't whether Dr. Pemberton loves her cat. The question is whether love is a sufficient basis for managing a potential existential threat."

Many people looking uncertain now. Hostile person winning.

Claire looked around the room. The committee members who had seemed sympathetic moments ago were now studying Harwick's folders, their expressions troubled. Even the Deputy Minister was nodding slowly.

"Dr. Pemberton," he said, not unkindly, "Mr. Harwick raises valid concerns. Your attachment to the animal is clear, and I don't doubt your sincerity. But this committee has a responsibility to consider all factors."

"The cat's well-being is one of those factors," Claire said desperately. "He needs me. The research shows—"

"The research is preliminary," Harwick interrupted. "And conducted by people who have already formed emotional attachments to the outcome. Minister Warren, I move that we table Options Two and Three pending further study, and implement Option Four as an interim measure. Sixty days of secure observation, full veterinary care, supervised visitation for Dr. Pemberton. After sixty days, we reconvene with actual data instead of assumptions."

Sixty days. Sixty days away from food lady. No. No no no.

Mungus's distress was becoming visible. The northern lights effect around him intensified, and the conference table began to vibrate slightly. Harwick's tablet finally gave up entirely, its screen cracking with a small pop.

"The entity's agitation," Harwick said, his voice rising slightly to be heard over the growing hum, "demonstrates exactly why we need professional handlers. Dr. Pemberton cannot control it. She can barely control herself."

"That's not fair," Agent Martinez said. "She's being ambushed—"

"She's being evaluated," Harwick corrected. "And she's failing. Minister Warren, I call for a vote."

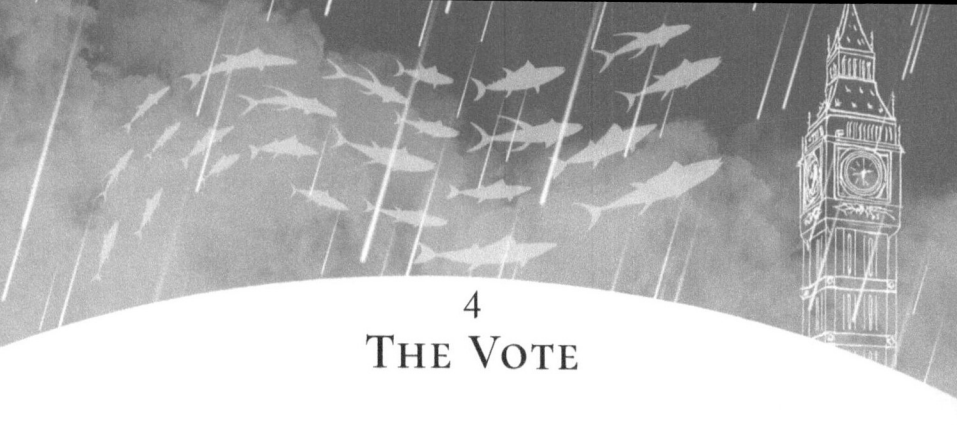

4
THE VOTE

"Courage is not the absence of fear. Courage is a cat walking into a cage to protect the person he loves."

The Deputy Minister looked around the room, then sighed with the weariness of a man who wanted nothing more than to be somewhere else. "All those in favor of Option Four as an interim measure?"

Claire watched, frozen, as hands went up around the table.

The Deputy Minister raised his first. Not enthusiastically—reluctantly, even apologetically—but his hand went up nonetheless. Claire's breath stopped and she couldn't look away from his raised hand.

The representative from the Home Office followed, a pinch-faced woman named Davidson who had been nodding along with Harwick's presentation. Her hand rose with the crisp efficiency of someone who had already decided before the meeting began.

Two hands. Bad. Very bad.

The woman from the Health and Safety Executive hesitated. Claire caught her eye and saw a flicker of sympathy—but then the woman's gaze flickered to Harwick's confident expression, and her hand rose too.

Three hands now. Food lady smells like fear now. Sharp fear.

The representative from Housing raised his hand without looking at anyone, staring at his documents as if eye contact might make him complicit in something he wasn't entirely comfortable with. Four.

Four. Too many. Make them stop.

Then the youngest member of the committee—a junior liaison from the Foreign Office named Peters who couldn't have been more than thirty—slowly raised his hand. He looked sick about it, actually pale, but his hand was up.

Five.

"All opposed?"

Agent Martinez's hand shot up immediately, fiercely, as if she could counterbalance the other five through sheer intensity. Claire felt a rush of gratitude so strong it almost made her dizzy.

Dr. Crumpet raised her hand with the measured dignity of someone who had faced down bureaucratic stupidity many times before and knew exactly how to make her displeasure clear.

The representative from DEFRA—the Department for Environment, Food and Rural Affairs—hesitated longest. He was a round-faced man named Thompson who had been watching Mungus throughout the meeting with what might have been genuine interest. Claire saw him look at Mungus, then at her, then at Harwick's smug expression.

His hand rose. Slowly, deliberately, defiantly.

Three opposed. It wasn't enough.

"Motion carries, five to three," the Deputy Minister announced, already packing up his documents, clearly eager to escape the tension in the room. "Option Four will be implemented as an interim measure. Dr. Pemberton, I'm sorry. This isn't a permanent decision—it's a precaution."

No. This cannot be. They cannot take me from food lady.

The word 'precaution' landed. Claire heard it echo through her mind, bouncing off memories of every committee meeting she'd ever attended, every academic review board that had dismissed her work, every time authority had chosen the safe option over the right one.

But this wasn't about her thesis. This wasn't about academic approval. This was about Mungus.

No. No. They're taking me from food lady. Must do something. Must fight.

The room exploded with cosmic interference.

Every screen in the conference room blazed to life, displaying cat videos at maximum volume—kittens playing with yarn, cats startled by cucumbers, a particularly fat tabby failing to jump onto a counter. The fluorescent lights began strobing through colors that definitely weren't in the standard spectrum: ultraviolet, infrared, colors that made people's eyes water because human brains weren't designed to process them.

The motivational posters on the walls cycled through increasingly desperate messages. "HANG IN THERE" became "EVERYTHING IS FINE" became "THIS IS A MISTAKE" became "PLEASE RECONSIDER" became "HE

NEEDS HER" became something in a script that no one could read but everyone somehow understood.

MAKE THEM UNDERSTAND. MAKE THEM SEE.

"Security protocol seven," Harwick spoke into his phone without raising his voice. He had prepared for this too. Of course he had. "We have a manifestation event. Initiate containment."

Strange people coming in. Carrying boxes. Dark boxes. Bad boxes.

Two technicians in grey jumpsuits entered carrying an oversized cat carrier constructed from light-absorbing materials. Runes were etched into its surface—not for show, Claire realized with horror, but for function. This was a cosmic dampening cage. They had been ready for this. They had been waiting for it.

The technicians moved toward Mungus with the practiced efficiency of people who had done this before, probably many times, probably to other cosmic beings whose owners had fought and lost.

"No!" Claire lunged forward, putting herself between the technicians and her cat. Her body moved before her mind could catch up, driven by something deeper than thought. "You can't just—this isn't—he's scared, can't you see that? He's not dangerous, he's *scared*."

"Dr. Pemberton, please step aside," one of the technicians said. His voice wasn't cruel—it was tired. The voice of someone who had heard variations of this speech before and knew how it ended. "This will be easier for everyone if you cooperate."

"I won't cooperate. I won't let you take him."

"Then we'll have to escort you out," Harwick said, and

there was a note of satisfaction in his voice now, hidden beneath professional concern. "Which will only distress the entity further. Is that what you want?"

Food lady crying. Food lady's face wet. Food lady NEVER cries.

Mungus had been watching all of this from his position on the conference table, his cosmic field roiling with distress. But at the sight of Claire's tears—tears she hadn't even realized were falling.

If food lady fights, they will hurt food lady. They will take food lady away. Cannot let them hurt food lady.

Must protect food lady. Even if it means...

His cosmic effects suddenly contracted, pulling inward like a held breath. The lights stopped strobing. The screens went dark. The motivational posters froze on their final message: "TRUST."

For a moment, the room was completely silent.

Have to be brave. Like food lady taught me. Brave means doing scary things anyway.

Then Mungus walked forward, away from Claire, toward the containment carrier.

"Mungus, no—" Claire's voice cracked. She reached for him, but Agent Martinez caught her arm with a grip that was both gentle and absolutely firm.

"Don't," Martinez whispered urgently. "If you interfere physically, they can have you arrested. Then you won't be able to fight this at all. You won't be able to visit. You won't be able to file appeals. They'll have won completely."

"I can't let them take him. I can't just watch—"

"You can't stop them. Not today. Not like this." Martinez's eyes were fierce. "But this isn't over. This is the beginning."

Going into dark box now. Smells like fear and old magic. Smells like other creatures who were scared.

Don't want to go in. Want to stay with food lady. But food lady must stay safe. Food lady must stay free.

This is how I protect her. By going.

Mungus stepped into the containment carrier with all the dignity he could muster. His paws didn't want to cooperate—they wanted to run, to fight, to claw at the technicians who were taking him away. But he made them walk. One step. Two steps. Three steps.

The carrier floor was cold.

The walls pressed in.

But he could still see food lady through the reinforced mesh, and that would have to be enough.

Will wait. Food lady will come. Food lady always comes.

This is what I believe. This is what I choose to believe.

As the door closed behind him, the last thing he saw was Claire's face—tear-streaked, devastated, but with fury building behind the tears.

She is already planning. Good. Food lady's plans are always good.

Will wait for food lady's plan.

"Dr. Pemberton," Harwick said, straightening his tie, "you'll receive documentation regarding visitation protocols within twenty-four hours. The facility is quite comfortable, I'm told. Your cat will be well cared for."

She couldn't speak. She couldn't move.

"This meeting is adjourned," the Deputy Minister announced, already packing up his documents.

The committee members filed out quickly, avoiding Claire's eyes. The representative from Housing actually ran, his documents clutched to his chest like a shield against guilt.

Only Agent Martinez and Dr. Crumpet remained.

The conference room felt enormous now, empty of everyone except the three of them and the echoing absence of one cosmically significant cat. The motivational posters had returned to their normal messages, but somehow "TEAMWORK MAKES THE DREAM WORK" felt mocking.

"I'm so sorry," Martinez said quietly, moving to sit beside Claire. "I didn't know he was going to do that. The personal attacks, the pre-lobbying, the vote—it was orchestrated. He must have been working on those committee members for days before the meeting even started."

"I should have seen it coming." Claire's voice sounded strange to her own ears. Hollow. Distant. Like it belonged to someone else. "I was so focused on defending Mungus that I didn't think about defending myself."

"That's not your fault. That's his strategy." Martinez's fingers whitened on the arm of her chair. "He attacks the person to discredit the argument. Makes it about you instead of about the cat. It's effective because it's cruel, and most people don't expect cruelty in a professional setting."

"Most people haven't met Gerald Harwick," Dr. Crumpet said dryly. She was still seated at the conference table, her temporal spectacles pushed up on her forehead, looking older than she had at the start of the meeting. "I've seen him use those tactics before. In the Sullivan case, in '08. And the Morrison incident three years later. He finds vulnerabilities and exploits them. It's his specialty."

"What happened in those cases?" Claire asked.

Dr. Crumpet was quiet for a long moment. "The entities were contained. Permanently. Neither ever returned to their companions."

The words hit Claire hard. She actually swayed, would have fallen if Martinez hadn't steadied her.

"But that's not going to happen here," Dr. Crumpet continued firmly. "Because those companions gave up. They accepted the committee's decision and walked away. They didn't fight."

"Can we fight? Can we really?" Her voice came out ragged. She didn't care. "The vote was five to three. The decision stands for sixty days. By then—"

"By then, we'll have built a case so strong that even Harwick won't be able to argue against it. He made a mistake today. Several mistakes, actually."

"What mistakes? He won."

"He won the battle. But he won it by cheating." Martinez pulled out her phone, scrolling through notes she must have been taking during the meeting. "He accessed your medical records without authorization. That's a GDPR violation. He cited research without proper attribution. He dismissed Dr. Crumpet's expertise without scientific basis. He pre-lobbied committee members before the formal meeting, which is against about seven different procedural rules."

"Will any of that matter?"

"It will matter because it's documented." Martinez looked up. "Harold?"

The demon emerged from behind his typewriter, where he had been typing throughout the entire exchange with the quiet dedication of someone recording history.

"I have everything," Harold said softly. "Every word. Every procedural violation. Every moment where Mr. Harwick bent or broke the rules to get what he wanted." He held up his typed pages—dozens of them, dense with text. "This is the beginning of his undoing, Dr. Pemberton. I promise you that."

Dark box. Quiet. Alone. Food lady's scent is here. Keep scent. Don't lose scent.

Somewhere across London, in a containment facility Mungus had never seen before, he lay curled in the corner of a too-clean room, trying to find the missing scent of a threadbare blue blanket that smelled like home.

But he wasn't giving up. Food lady was fighting. He could feel it somehow, across the distance—her fierce determination, her rising anger, her refusal to accept defeat.

Outside his window, the London skyline flickered briefly with aurora light that shouldn't have been visible from the ground. Mungus watched it pulse—Loss? Anger? He couldn't tell anymore—then tucked his nose beneath his paw and closed his eyes.

Will wait. Food lady will come.

Food lady always comes.

5
THE DEPARTMENT OF INCREASINGLY FRANTIC SOLUTIONS

"When faced with an impossible problem, humans have two choices: accept that it cannot be solved, or form another committee to prove it can. The third choice—letting a graduate student and a demon drown the opposition in paperwork—is rarely considered, but often most effective."

> @BBCBreaking BREAKING: Meteorological anomalies intensify over London. Third fish shower in two weeks. Government denies connection to "Containment Facility Alpha." #FishShower #DoomsdayCat

> @ConspiracyChronicles THREAD: The cosmic cat is in a CAGE and reality is BREAKING. Connect the dots: fish showers up 400%, traffic lights speaking dead languages, my microwave keeps showing me next week's lottery numbers (they're wrong btw). The cat is ANGRY. 🧵 1/67

CNN International chyron: "COSMIC CAT CONTAINMENT: IS BRITAIN'S SOLUTION MAKING THINGS WORSE?"

> Le Monde headline: "Le Chat Cosmique Britannique: Captivité Controversée"

@QuantumPhysicsMemes when the government puts your reality-warping cat in jail and now it rains fish every Tuesday [image: London skyline with fish falling] 287k likes

> The Guardian Opinion: The Ethics of Cosmic Containment—Are We Torturing a Cat to Balance the Budget? By Prof. Eleanor Whitmore

@TikTokUser2843 Day 18 of cosmic containment and my traffic light just displayed "FREE MUNGUS" in ancient Sumerian. I don't even know Sumerian but I KNOW that's what it said. The vibes are OFF. #FreeMungus #DoomsdayCat

> Financial Times headline: "Reality Fluctuations Triple Since Cat Containment; Treasury Maintains Decision Was 'Fiscally Sound'"

Reddit: r/UnresolvedMysteries [Megathread] Containment Facility Alpha: Location theories, leaked documents, and why the fish showers are getting worse

> @Number10Press The Prime Minister has received formal inquiries from 34 world leaders regarding the UK's "cosmic cat situation." An international conference has been scheduled. Statement to follow.

Day 5 of Containment

The first visitation had been the hardest.

Claire had arrived at Containment Facility Alpha with her heart in her throat and her hands shaking so badly she'd dropped her visitor badge twice. The security protocols had taken forty-five minutes—forms to sign, equipment to surrender, a briefing about "appropriate interaction parameters" that had made her want to scream.

And then they'd brought him in.

Food lady. FOOD LADY.

Mungus had thrown himself against the mesh of the reinforced carrier with such force that the handler had stumbled. His cosmic field flared wildly—the fluorescent lights exploded into aurora patterns, the security cameras began displaying what appeared to be ancient star maps, and somewhere in the building, every fire alarm started playing jazz.

"Mungus, hey, hey—" Claire had pressed her hands against the mesh, trying to calm him. "I'm here. I'm here. It's okay."

NOT okay. Want out. Want food lady. Want HOME.

"I know. I know, baby. But I can't—they won't let me—"

The handler had been kind about it, at least. "Dr.

Pemberton, you have thirty minutes. I'd recommend using them to help him settle, if you can. The calmer he is, the easier this will be for everyone."

Thirty minutes. They were giving her thirty minutes with her cat, who she'd spent every day with for three years, who slept on her chest and supervised her thesis writing and knocked things off tables just to watch them fall.

Why no home? Bad cat? Was I bad cat?

"You weren't bad," Claire had whispered, tears streaming down her face. "You were never bad. This isn't your fault. It's not anyone's fault except—" She'd stopped herself. Blaming Harwick wouldn't help. Nothing would help except getting Mungus out of there.

The thirty minutes had passed in what felt like seconds. When the handler returned to take Mungus away, his cosmic field had contracted into something small and dim, like a candle flame in a hurricane.

Food lady leaves. Again. Always leaving now. Sad.

"I'll be back," Claire had promised, her voice breaking. "Every day. I'll be back every single day until you come home."

Promise?

"Promise."

She had kept that promise. Every day for five days, she had navigated the security protocols and the paperwork and the pitying looks from staff members who clearly thought she was wasting her time. Every day, she had watched Mungus grow a little dimmer, a little more withdrawn, a little more convinced that this was his new reality.

And every day, she had promised him it wouldn't last forever.

She just wished she believed it.

Day 12 of Containment

"I found something," Harold announced, his small demon face glowing with excitement.

Claire looked up from the legal brief she'd been reading for the third time, trying to find angles that weren't there. It was past midnight. Martinez had gone home hours ago, but Claire couldn't sleep—every time she closed her eyes, she saw Mungus pressing against the mesh, his cosmic field dimming.

"What kind of something?"

"The kind of something that could change everything." Harold produced a document written on what looked like actual parchment. "The 1847 Prophetic Parrot Precedent. I mentioned it before, but I've found the complete ruling."

Claire took the document carefully. The handwriting was elaborate and difficult to read, but Harold had attached a typed translation.

"'The bond between a cosmically significant entity and its primary companion,'" she read aloud, "'constitutes not merely an emotional preference but a fundamental requirement for stable integration of supernatural abilities. To sever such a bond is not merely cruel but practically dangerous, as the entity's powers will inevitably destabilize without the anchoring presence of their chosen human.'"

"Keep reading," Harold urged.

"'It is therefore the judgment of this tribunal that the prophetic parrot known as Cassandra shall be returned forthwith to the custody of one Margaret Beaumont, her owner of seven years, and that no future attempt shall be made to separate them on grounds of public safety, as such separation itself constitutes the greater threat to public safety.'"

Claire stared at the document. "This is from 1847. This is binding precedent?"

"International supernatural law operates on different principles than mundane law," Harold explained, practically bouncing with enthusiasm. "Older precedents carry *more* weight, not less. And look—the ruling was made by a tribunal that included representatives from France, Germany, and the Ottoman Empire. It's not just British law. It's international."

"Does Harwick know about this?"

"Harwick knows about budgets and procedures. He doesn't know about the Prophetic Parrot Precedent because he didn't think to look for it." Harold's eyes gleamed. "But I did. Because proper research is a form of love, Dr. Pemberton, and I love paperwork very, very much."

For the first time in twelve days, Claire felt the first stirrings of hope.

Day 15 of Containment

"We're building something," Claire told Mungus through the mesh. "A case. A real case, with evidence and precedents and—"

Don't understand case. Food lady's sounds are... strong now. Good strong.

"I sound different because I'm not giving up. I know I seemed—I know the first few visits were hard. I was scared. I didn't know what to do." She pressed her palm against the mesh, feeling the warmth of his nose on the other side. "But I've got a team now. Martinez found procedural violations. Harold found a legal precedent from 1847. Professor Blackwood is going to testify about the science."

Many mouth sounds. Don't understand. But food lady's heart beats differently. Faster. Stronger.

"We're going to win," Claire said, and for the first time, she believed it. "We're going to win, and you're going to come home, and I'm going to spend the rest of my life making sure no one ever puts you in a box again."

Mungus's cosmic field flickered—not with uncertainty, but with a brightness that was almost hope.

Food lady making plan. Food lady always has plans. Good plans.

"The best plan," Claire agreed. "The best plan I've ever made."

Outside the visitation room, it began to rain. Not fish—just rain. Clean, ordinary, completely normal rain.

The first normal weather London had seen in two weeks.

Day 19 of Containment

The visitation room at Containment Facility Alpha was painted the same institutional beige as every other government building Claire had encountered, but someone had made an effort. There were plants—real ones, not plastic—and a window that looked out onto a small courtyard garden. The chairs were actually comfortable.

None of it mattered.

Food lady here. Food lady here. Food lady HERE.

Mungus pressed against the mesh of the reinforced carrier they brought him in for visits, his entire body vibrating with a purr that made the fluorescent lights flicker and the plants lean toward him like sunflowers toward the sun.

"Hey, you," Claire whispered, sliding her fingers through the mesh to scratch behind his ears. "I'm here. I'm always here."

Scratches. Good scratches. Not enough scratches. Want to go home with food lady.

Through the mesh, she could see that his fur had lost some of its luster. Not dramatically—they were taking good care of him physically—but there was a dimness to him that hadn't been there before. The aurora effects that used to dance around him constantly were muted, flickering uncertainly like a candle in a draft.

"The cosmic readings are concerning," Dr. Crumpet had told her yesterday, her voice gentle but honest. "His power levels are actually increasing—the fish showers prove that—but his stability is decreasing. He's becoming more powerful and less controlled simultaneously. It's exactly what we predicted would happen if the bond was disrupted."

Claire had asked what that meant long-term.

Dr. Crumpet had been quiet for a long moment before answering: "It means Mr. Harwick's 'fiscally responsible' solution may end up costing considerably more than two million pounds annually. Possibly in the form of London becoming permanently unstable."

Food lady smells like worry and coffee and not enough sleep. Food lady not taking care of herself.

"I've been working on our case," Claire told him, keeping her voice steady even though her heart was breaking. "Martinez found a procedural argument—Harwick used confidential medical records without proper authorization. That's grounds for appeal. And Harold has been going through every regulation about supernatural entity custody. Did you know there's a 1847 precedent about a prophetic parrot? The owner won custody back on grounds of 'emotional interdependence.' We're citing it."

Don't understand mouth sounds. Understand food lady is fighting. Good food lady.

Mungus pushed harder against the mesh, and Claire felt something wet on her fingers. She looked down to find that the mesh where he was pressing had begun to glow faintly gold—not melting, exactly, but softening somehow. Responding to his need.

"Don't," she whispered urgently. "If they see you affecting the containment, they'll use it as evidence that you're dangerous. They'll make the restrictions worse."

Want to go home. Want cardboard box. Want food lady's lap.

The glow faded reluctantly. Claire felt tears sliding down her cheeks and didn't bother to wipe them away.

"Eighteen more days until the international conference," she said. "That's our chance. Forty-one days left in the containment order, but we're not waiting that long. We're going to win, and you're going to come home, and I'm going to buy you the most expensive tuna in London. The kind that costs more than my student loans."

Tuna sounds good. Home sounds better. Food lady sounds best.

"Time's up, Dr. Pemberton." The guard's voice was apologetic but firm.

Claire pressed her palm flat against the mesh, and Mungus pressed his face against it from the other side. For a moment, just a moment, the barrier seemed to disappear entirely, and she could feel his fur against her skin.

Will wait. Food lady will win. Food lady always wins.

"I love you," she whispered. "I'm coming back for you."

Know. Always know.

As they carried him away, the lights in the facility flickered once—not with interference, but with something that felt almost like a goodbye wave.

Outside, it began to rain fish.

Day 21 of Containment

"The international pressure is mounting," Agent Martinez said, spreading documents across Claire's kitchen table—the same table where Mungus had eaten the Seal of Final Things and started this whole impossible situation. "Thirty-four countries have formally requested observer status at the conference. The UN has appointed a Special Rapporteur for Cosmic Entity Rights. And someone started a Change.org petition to grant Mungus political asylum in Iceland."

"Iceland?" Claire asked, not looking up from the legal brief she was annotating. She hadn't slept more than four hours a night since the containment order, surviving on coffee and a desperate need to be doing *something*.

"Apparently they've decided cosmic cats align well with their national values. Something about respecting the unknowable." Martinez shrugged. "The point is, Harwick's 'quiet domestic solution' has become an international incident. That gives us leverage."

The forms creature has found seventeen procedural violations, Harold's voice came from the corner, where he had set up what could only be described as a war room of paperwork. Stacks of documents surrounded him like fortifications, cross-referenced with color-coded tabs and connected by strings of red yarn that made the whole setup look like a conspiracy theorist's fever dream. "Seventeen! And that's just in the original committee meeting. If we include the containment order itself, I'm up to thirty-four."

"Will any of them stick?" Claire asked.

"The medical records violation is the strongest," Martinez said. "Harwick accessed your university health records without proper authorization. That's a clear breach of GDPR and several internal Ministry protocols. It won't overturn the containment on its own, but it undermines his credibility and gives us grounds to request that his recommendation be struck from the record."

Claire set down her pen. "What about the science? Can we prove that containing Mungus is making things worse?"

"Dr. Crumpet has been compiling the data." Martinez pulled out a thick folder. "Cosmic event frequency has tripled since containment began. The fish showers alone have caused an estimated two million pounds in property damage—ironic, given that was exactly the annual budget

Harwick was trying to avoid. And the readings from Mungus himself show clear signs of stress-induced instability."

"He's getting worse because he's not with me," Claire said quietly.

"That's exactly what the data shows. And that's our strongest argument." Martinez met her eyes. "The containment isn't just cruel, Claire. It's counterproductive. It's making the exact problem Harwick claimed to be solving demonstrably worse. We can prove, with hard numbers, that his solution has failed."

For the first time in three weeks, Claire felt something like hope.

"How do we present this?"

"That's what we need to figure out." Martinez pulled up a chair. "The international conference is our one shot. Every major power will have representatives there. If we can convince them that the UK's approach has failed and that your bond with Mungus is the actual stabilizing factor, we can get an international recommendation to overturn the domestic decision."

"Harwick will fight it."

"Harwick will *try* to fight it. But he's going to be defending a policy that has objectively made things worse, in front of an international audience that's already skeptical of him. He's not in a strong position, even if he doesn't know it yet."

Harold looked up from his forms, his small demon face bright with enthusiasm. "I've also discovered something wonderful. The 1923 International Convention on Supernatural Entity Welfare—which the UK signed but apparently forgot about—includes provisions requiring that 'the emotional and psychological needs of cosmically significant beings shall be given equal weight to practical considerations of public safety.' Harwick never cited it in his assessment. That's another procedural violation."

"How many does that make?" Claire asked.

"Thirty-five." Harold was practically glowing. "We're going to bury him in paperwork. It's going to be *beautiful*."

Day 25 of Containment

"You look terrible," Professor Blackwood said, not unkindly, as Claire sat across from him in his cluttered office at the university.

"I haven't been sleeping," she admitted. "Every time I close my eyes, I see him in that carrier. Pressing against the mesh."

Blackwood nodded slowly. "I came to apologize. When this started, I treated the Seal as an academic curiosity. I should have warned you more clearly about the risks of keeping cosmic artifacts near domestic animals."

"Would it have mattered? Mungus eats everything. He once ate a shoe."

"Perhaps not." Blackwood almost smiled. "But I also should have prepared you for what would come next. The bureaucracy, the committees, the people who would see your cat as a problem to be solved rather than a being to be protected. That's my world, Claire. I should have guided you through it from the start."

"You're here now."

"I am." He leaned forward. "And I want to help. I've been

reviewing the research on cosmic entity bonds, and I believe I can offer expert testimony at the international conference. The data supporting your connection to Mungus is substantial. It's not just sentiment—it's measurable, quantifiable, scientifically significant."

Claire felt tears threatening again. "Why are you doing this?"

"Because you were right, that first day. When you told Agent Martinez that Mungus wasn't a problem to be solved. That he was family." Blackwood's voice was gruff. "I've spent my career studying the impossible. But I'd forgotten that the impossible often comes with emotional stakes. That it matters to someone." He paused. "You reminded me of that."

"Professor—"

"Also," he added, with the ghost of a smile, "I've grown rather fond of the cat videos he keeps putting on my computer. The one with the kittens and the cucumbers is genuinely amusing."

Even far away, can still improve hostile-adjacent person's computer. Good skill.

Three days until the conference. Three days to turn thirty-five procedural violations into a weapon. Three days to bring Mungus home.

Claire closed the folder, squared its edges against the table, and reached for the next one.

6
THE INTERNATIONAL CONFERENCE

"Truth has a way of surfacing, even in rooms designed to bury it. Especially when assisted by a cat who has learned to type."

Day 28 of Containment: The International Conference

The conference room was larger than the one where Claire had lost the first vote, with screens connecting representatives from seven countries and observer delegations from a dozen more. The setup was professional, intimidating, and clearly designed for high-stakes international diplomacy.

Claire sat at the UK delegation's table, flanked by Agent Martinez and Professor Blackwood. Harold had been given official status as a "consulting administrative entity" and was positioned at a small desk with his typewriter, ready to document everything. Dr. Crumpet appeared on the main screen, attending from three temporal locations simultaneously.

Across the room, Gerald Harwick sat with a team of Treasury officials, looking confident. He had new documents, new presentations, new arguments. He had spent the last four weeks preparing his defense.

But Claire had spent four weeks preparing too.

"Ladies and gentlemen," the chairperson announced—a stern woman from the UN's Department of Impossible Situations whose nameplate read "Director Okonkwo"—"we are here to review the United Kingdom's handling of the FRCE-A7 event known informally as 'the Doomsday Cat.' Specifically, we will consider whether the current containment approach should continue, or whether alternative management strategies should be implemented."

Director Okonkwo's gaze swept the room with the authority of someone who had adjudicated disputes between supernatural entities and nation-states, and found both equally tiresome.

"I will remind all parties that this is a fact-finding session, not a debate. We are here to determine what is true, not what is convenient. Mr. Harwick, as the architect of the current policy, you may present first."

Many people. Important meeting. Food lady far away but can feel food lady fighting. Good.

Harwick stood, straightening his tie with the practiced confidence of someone who had never lost an argument he'd properly prepared for. "Madam Director, the UK's approach has been cautious, measured, and fiscally responsible. We implemented a sixty-day observation period to gather data before making permanent decisions. This is standard protocol for cosmic anomalies of unknown—"

"Mr. Harwick," Director Okonkwo interrupted, "the data

we've received suggests that cosmic disturbances have increased significantly since containment began. Can you explain this?"

"Minor fluctuations are to be expected during any adjustment period—"

"Fish showers have increased by four hundred percent." The voice came from the German representative, a precise man named Dr. Weber who had been reviewing data on his tablet. "Traffic infrastructure across London has begun displaying messages in dead languages. Three separate incidents of temporal displacement have been recorded in the past week alone." He looked up. "These are not minor fluctuations, Mr. Harwick. These are significant escalations."

Harwick's confidence flickered, but he recovered quickly. "The entity's instability demonstrates precisely why containment was necessary. Imagine if these disturbances were occurring in an unsecured civilian environment—"

"The disturbances *were* occurring in an unsecured civilian environment," Agent Martinez interjected. "For weeks before containment. At significantly lower levels. Dr. Crumpet?"

Dr. Crumpet's image stabilized on screen, her temporal spectacles showing data that seemed to exist in multiple timeframes simultaneously. "I can confirm that cosmic event frequency was approximately seventy percent lower while the cat remained with Dr. Pemberton. The data is quite clear: containment has not reduced instability. It has dramatically increased it."

The Japanese representative, a woman named Dr. Tanaka who specialized in entity-human bonds, leaned forward. "Dr. Crumpet, in your professional opinion, is this escalation reversible? If the cat were returned to Dr. Pemberton's care, would we see a return to previous stability levels?"

"Based on our models, yes. The bond between a cosmic entity and its primary companion functions as a stabilizing anchor. Disrupting that bond has predictable negative consequences. Restoring it should have equally predictable positive ones."

"Should," Harwick said quickly. "Not 'will.' We're being asked to make policy based on theoretical projections."

"Mr. Harwick," Dr. Tanaka said coolly, "your containment policy was also based on theoretical projections. The difference is that yours have proven incorrect, while Dr. Crumpet's have been validated by four weeks of observable data."

Directeur Beaumont from France leaned forward, her expression calculating. "Is it possible the instability is a natural progression, unrelated to containment?"

"Possible but unlikely," Dr. Crumpet replied. "Our models consistently show correlation between the cat's emotional state and cosmic output. The cat is distressed because it has been separated from its primary companion. The distress manifests as cosmic instability. This is not speculation—it is measurable."

"Then the solution," Harwick said quickly, pivoting, "is to find a different primary companion. Someone more suitable. A trained professional rather than an anxious graduate student with—"

"Mr. Harwick." Claire's voice cut through the room like a blade. She hadn't planned to speak yet, but she couldn't let that go. Not again. "You're about to reference my medical records again. The ones you accessed without authorization."

The room went quiet.

"I have documentation," Claire continued, her voice steady despite the way her heart was pounding, "showing that you obtained my university health records without going through proper data protection channels. Harold?"

Harold produced a folder with the flourish of someone who had been waiting weeks for this moment. "Form DP-7: Notice of Unauthorized Data Access. Form GDPR-12: Complaint of Privacy Violation. Form HR-94: Request for Disciplinary Review. All filed and acknowledged."

"Additionally," Harold continued, warming to his subject, "Form IP-23: Violation of the 1923 International Convention on Supernatural Entity Welfare, which requires that emotional and psychological needs of cosmically significant beings be given equal weight to practical considerations. This convention was never cited in Mr. Harwick's assessment. Form PR-8: Citation of the 1847 Prophetic Parrot Precedent, which establishes binding international law regarding the inseverability of cosmic entity bonds—"

"That's quite enough forms for now, Harold," Director Okonkwo said, though there was a hint of amusement in her voice. "Mr. Harwick, these are serious allegations. Do you have a response?"

Harwick's face had gone pale, then red. "Those records were relevant to assessing suitability—"

"My mental health history," Claire said, "has no bearing on my ability to care for a cat. What it *does* have bearing on is your credibility as someone who will follow proper procedures. You broke the rules to win an argument, Mr.

Harwick. How can this committee trust that you followed proper procedures in everything else?"

"This is a distraction from the actual issue—"

"The actual issue," Claire pressed on, standing now, addressing the full room, "is that your containment policy has failed. Not theoretically. Not hypothetically. *Actually.* The data proves it. Dr. Crumpet has shown that cosmic disturbances have tripled. The fish showers alone have cost more than the annual budget you were trying to save. Your 'fiscally responsible' solution has been *expensive*, Mr. Harwick. And it's going to get more expensive every day that cat stays in containment."

The Australian representative, a weathered man named Davies who had been listening with growing amusement, spoke up. "So what you're telling us is that the cheapest, safest, and most effective solution... is to give the cat back to the graduate student?"

"That is precisely what the data suggests," Dr. Crumpet confirmed.

"Well," Davies said, leaning back with a slight smile, "that's rather inconvenient for Mr. Harwick's position, isn't it?"

Laughter rippled through some of the delegations. Harwick's team was looking increasingly uncomfortable.

Directeur Beaumont tried again. "Even if we accept that the bond is important, surely we cannot simply—"

Food lady winning. Food lady fighting. Can feel it. Can feel hope.

Want to help. Want to help food lady.

The screens around the room flickered.

At first, it was subtle—a slight shimmer, easily dismissed

as a technical glitch. But then Harwick's presentation slides began changing. His carefully prepared charts and graphs started displaying different data: the actual comparative statistics showing cosmic disturbances before and after containment. His cost-benefit analysis suddenly included the two million pounds in fish shower damage he'd neglected to mention.

"What—" Harwick stabbed at his laptop. "This isn't—someone is tampering with—"

Make screens show food lady's feeling. Show the strong feeling.

"Mr. Harwick," the chairperson said slowly, "are these figures accurate?"

"They—the presentation has been—"

"The figures are accurate," Dr. Crumpet confirmed, a hint of amusement in her voice. "It seems the entity is contributing to the proceedings."

On every screen in the room, a simple message appeared: **I WANT TO GO HOME.**

Then, below it: **PLEASE.**

The room was absolutely silent.

Food lady crying. Happy crying? Hope so. Want to go home to food lady.

"Well," the Australian representative said quietly, "I don't think I've ever seen a more compelling witness statement."

Claire was crying now—not from sadness, but from overwhelming relief and love and pride. Mungus, from wherever he was in containment, had found a way to speak for himself. Not by attacking his opponents, but by simply asking for what he needed.

I MISS HER.

The words hung on every screen, glowing softly.

Directeur Beaumont's expression had shifted from skepticism to genuine emotion. "The creature is... making a request?"

"The *cat*," Agent Martinez corrected firmly, "is telling you that containment is hurting him. And the data supports his statement."

The chairperson looked around the room. "I believe we've heard enough. This committee will now vote on whether to recommend immediate termination of the containment order and implementation of Option Three: permanent co-habitation management with Dr. Pemberton as primary caretaker."

Harwick made one last attempt. "This is exactly the kind of emotional manipulation we should be guarding against. The entity is clearly capable of influencing technology—how can we trust any decision made under its influence?"

"Mr. Harwick," the chairperson said coolly, "the cat didn't change your data. It *revealed* your data. There's a difference." She turned to the room. "All in favor of terminating containment?"

Hands went up around the room. The Australian. The German representative. Japan. Canada. Brazil. Even Directeur Beaumont, after a long moment, raised her hand.

"All opposed?"

Harwick's hand went up. His Treasury team followed. No one else.

"Motion carries. The containment order is terminated effective immediately. Mr. Harwick, I suggest you begin preparing an explanation for why your department's 'fiscally responsible' solution cost more in four weeks than Option Three would have cost in a year."

The screens around the room cleared, then displayed one final message:

THANK YOU.

And then, in smaller letters below:

ALSO I'M HUNGRY.

The Reunion

They released him an hour later.

Claire stood in the courtyard of Containment Facility Alpha, her heart pounding so hard she could feel it in her throat. The day had turned golden, late afternoon sun slanting through clouds that seemed to be arranging themselves into particularly aesthetic formations. Agent Martinez stood beside her, along with Professor Blackwood, Harold, and what was surely half the Ministry staff, all of whom had found excuses to witness this moment.

"They're coming," Martinez said quietly, watching the facility doors.

Claire couldn't speak. Her throat had closed up entirely.

The doors opened, and a handler emerged carrying a standard cat carrier—no reinforced mesh this time, no cosmic dampening technology, no symbols etched into the surface. Just a regular carrier with a regular door.

Inside, she could see movement. A pair of golden-green eyes catching the light.

FOOD LADY. FOOD LADY. FOOD LADY.

The handler set the carrier down and reached for the latch. "Dr. Pemberton, I should warn you, he's been quite—"

She didn't hear the rest. The door opened, and Mungus shot out like a small furry missile launched from a catapult. He hit Claire at approximately chest height and clung there, all four paws gripping her jacket, his face buried in her neck, purring so loudly that every window in the building began vibrating in harmony.

Home. Home. Food lady. HOME.

"I've got you," Claire sobbed, wrapping her arms around him so tightly she was probably squishing him. He didn't seem to mind. If anything, he pressed closer, as if trying to merge with her entirely. "I've got you. You're coming home. You're never going back there. Never. I promise. Never again."

Never leaving food lady. Never. Never never never.

The courtyard erupted.

Not with applause—though there was some of that—but with light. The aurora effects that had been dim and uncertain for weeks exploded outward in a cascade of color that made several observers gasp and one junior analyst burst into tears. Golds and greens and purples danced through the air, weaving patterns that seemed to spell out words in languages that didn't exist yet, that might never exist, that existed only in this moment of impossible joy.

So happy. Everything feels beautiful now.

The fish shower that had been threatening all morning —the clouds had had that particular tuna-scented heaviness —transformed mid-formation. Instead of temporally displaced seafood, flower petals began to drift down from a clear sky. Roses and lilies and flowers that botanists would later struggle to identify, all falling in gentle spirals around the reunion.

"The cosmic readings," Dr. Crumpet's voice came through Martinez's phone, audibly awed, "are already stabilizing. We're seeing a thirty percent reduction in anomalous events just from the past ten minutes. His field is... it's reorganizing itself. Settling into patterns we haven't seen since before containment."

"He's happy," Claire said, her face buried in Mungus's fur, tasting tears and cat hair and not caring about either. "He was always going to be okay if he was happy."

Happy. Happy. Never been so happy. Food lady smells like home. Food lady smells like forever.

Professor Blackwood cleared his throat, looking suspiciously bright-eyed himself. "I believe this validates my testimony rather thoroughly. The bond between them is clearly the stabilizing factor."

"Your testimony was excellent, Professor," Martinez said. "Though I think the cat's testimony was more persuasive."

Did help. Showed truth. Asked nicely. Food lady did rest.

"You did help," Claire whispered to him. "You helped so much. 'I want to go home. Please.' That was perfect. That was exactly right."

Learned from food lady. Food lady always says please helps.

Harold appeared at the facility entrance, clutching a truly impressive stack of paperwork. His small demon face was wet with what might have been tears, if demons cried, which they apparently did when sufficiently moved by proper documentation procedures.

"The Ministry of Unusual Pet Incidents and Related Concerns has been officially established!" he announced, his voice thick with emotion. "I have the founding documents right here. All forty-seven forms, organized by color and cross-referenced by subject. The first form creates the Ministry. The second form establishes Dr. Pemberton's position as Chief Cat Liaison. The third form officially recognizes the human-cosmic entity bond as a protected relationship under international law."

He held up the stack reverently.

"We did it. We created an entirely new category of bureaucracy. It's the most beautiful thing I've ever been part of."

Claire laughed—really laughed, freely and fully, for the first time in four weeks. The sound seemed to make the flower petals swirl in delighted spirals.

"Can I sign them later? Can I take my cat home first?"

"Oh, absolutely. The forms will keep. Forms are very patient." Harold beamed through his tears. "Besides, I suspect the cat's signature is going to be required on some of these, and I'm not entirely sure how to accomplish that yet. Perhaps a paw print? In cosmic ink? I'll need to research the precedents."

Will sign all forms. Will sign anything. Just want to go home with food lady.

As Claire carried Mungus toward Agent Martinez's car, the late afternoon sun caught the flower petals still drifting down around them, turning the whole scene into something out of a fairy tale. The kind of fairy tale where the happy ending wasn't given but earned, fought for, won through preparation and persistence and paperwork and an unshakeable belief that love was worth fighting for.

"You know," Martinez said, falling into step beside her,

"Harwick's computer is still showing nothing but cat videos. It's been like that for days. The IT department has tried everything."

Bad person gets cat pictures. Good.

"I'm sure he's learning a lot," Claire said.

From somewhere inside her jacket, pressed against her heart, Mungus purred his agreement. Around them, reality settled into something that felt like contentment—not perfect, not normal, but right in a way that nothing had felt right for twenty-eight days.

They were going home.

Finally. Finally. Finally.

Home.

7
THE ASK

"Trust, once broken, must be rebuilt one small choice at a time. The hardest part isn't the rebuilding—it's finding the courage to ask for it again."

Three Days After Reunion

Claire woke to find Mungus pressed against her chest, purring so loudly the windows were vibrating. This had become their new normal since his release—he refused to sleep anywhere but directly on top of her, as close as physically possible, as if afraid she might disappear if he couldn't feel her heartbeat.

Food lady still here. Good. Checking again. Still here.

She didn't mind. After twenty-eight days of sleeping alone, of lying awake imagining him in that sterile containment cell, she found his weight comforting rather than uncomfortable. The purring that once would have kept her awake now lulled her into the deepest sleep she'd had in months.

"Good morning, cosmic menace," she murmured, scratching behind his ears. The aurora effect that danced around him brightened in response, casting shifting colors across her bedroom ceiling.

Morning scratches. Best scratches. Never leaving food lady again.

But even as she savored the moment, Claire couldn't ignore what she'd been noticing for days.

It had started small. A flicker in his aurora effects during Tuesday's breakfast. A moment yesterday when his purr had skipped like a record with a scratch. She'd told herself it was nothing—adjustment, maybe, or lingering stress from containment. Cats took time to settle after trauma. Everyone said so.

Then, during what should have been a normal nap yesterday afternoon, he'd briefly become partially transparent.

She'd been reading on the couch, Mungus curled in his usual spot on her lap, when she'd looked down and seen the fabric of her jeans through his fur. Just for a moment—three seconds, maybe four—before he solidified again, still sleeping, apparently unaware that he'd briefly stopped being entirely present in this dimension.

Claire hadn't slept well since.

Stomach feels strange. Has felt strange since before. Getting stranger.

"You're not feeling well, are you?" she asked now, watching his face for any sign of the flickering she'd seen yesterday.

Feel fine. Feel mostly fine. Feel... strange.

He pressed closer against her, and she felt the heat radiating from his fur—warmer than usual, warmer than was probably healthy for a cat, cosmic or otherwise. When she ran her hand along his side, she could feel something underneath the purr. A vibration that didn't quite match the rhythm. Like an engine with a knock in it.

"We should call someone," she said, more to herself than to him. "Dr. Crumpet, maybe. Or Martinez. They'd know if this is normal."

Don't want strangers. Just got home. Want quiet. Want food lady.

"I know, baby. I know you just want to rest." She gathered him closer, feeling the irregular warmth of him against her chest. "Maybe it's nothing. Maybe you just need time."

Yes. Time. More time with food lady. Everything fine.

But even as she said it, she saw the aurora effects around him stutter and skip, cycling through colors that didn't quite connect to each other. And for just a moment—half a second, barely noticeable—she could see through his left ear.

Claire reached for her phone.

Agent Martinez arrived at nine with Dr. Crumpet, who was carrying monitoring equipment that seemed to exist in several time zones simultaneously. Claire had spent the hour since her call trying to pretend everything was normal—feeding Mungus his breakfast, tidying the flat, making tea that she'd let go cold without drinking.

"The dissolution is accelerating," Dr. Crumpet said without preamble, setting up devices that beeped with increasing urgency. "The separation trauma appears to have destabilized the artifact's integration with his system. Ironic, really—Mr. Harwick's containment may have turned a manageable situation into an urgent one."

Many beeping things. Don't like beeping things. Remind me of bad place.

Mungus retreated behind Claire's legs, watching the equipment with wary eyes. Since his release, he'd been nervous around anything that looked official or institutional—a learned fear that made Claire want to gather him up and run somewhere far from government buildings and cosmic monitoring devices.

"It's okay," she murmured, reaching down to stroke his back. "They're here to help. I promise."

Food lady says safe. Trusting food lady. But watching carefully.

"How urgent?" Claire asked, straightening up. "When you say accelerating—"

Dr. Crumpet consulted her temporal spectacles, which were displaying information that made her frown deepen. "Based on current trajectory, the artifact will achieve complete existential dissolution within forty-eight hours."

"Forty-eight hours." Claire heard her own voice go flat. "Two days."

"After that point, reality will begin reorganizing itself according to principles that... well, let's just say physics as we know it would become considerably more subjective."

"What does that mean? Specifically?"

Dr. Crumpet exchanged a look with Martinez before

answering. "It means gravity might become optional in certain neighborhoods. Time might flow in multiple directions simultaneously. The Thames could decide it prefers to flow uphill. These are not hypothetical concerns—they're projected outcomes based on the current rate of artifact deterioration."

Don't understand big words. Understand food lady getting more scared.

"What happens to Mungus?"

"The cat himself should survive the process. His system has integrated with the artifact sufficiently that the dissolution shouldn't harm him directly." Dr. Crumpet paused. "But 'survive' and 'remain unchanged' are different things. If we let the dissolution complete naturally, his cosmic abilities could become... unpredictable. Potentially dangerous. To himself as much as to anyone else."

Claire crouched down beside Mungus, running her hands through his fur. He leaned into her touch, purring his irregular purr, and she felt the heat radiating from him—definitely warmer than this morning. Definitely getting worse.

Food lady's hands feel nice. Food lady worried though. Can smell worry.

"There has to be something we can do," Claire said. "Some way to help him."

Martinez crouched down to Mungus's level, moving slowly. "Hey, little guy. I know you're nervous. But we're going to figure this out, okay? We're not going to let anything bad happen to you."

Official lady who helped food lady. Okay person. Still watching.

"We've contacted Dr. Elena Ramirez," Martinez continued, addressing Claire. "She specializes in supernatural veterinary procedures. She's dealt with ingested artifacts before—not quite on this scale, but she has relevant experience. She believes she can induce a controlled cosmic regurgitation."

"Regurgitation?"

"Basically helping Mungus expel the dissolving artifact naturally. Like a hairball, but with more cosmic significance."

Claire felt a flicker of hope. "That sounds... manageable. Is it safe?"

"Safer than the alternative," Dr. Crumpet said. "And considerably safer than the surgical intervention Mr. Harwick was advocating for. The procedure uses natural biological responses enhanced with mystical components. It works with the body rather than against it."

Body wants to do something. Stomach feels very strange. Maybe getting strange thing out would help.

"There's a complication, though," Martinez said carefully. "Dr. Ramirez will explain the details when she arrives, but I wanted to prepare you."

"Prepare me for what?"

Martinez hesitated. "The procedure requires physical stillness. Complete stillness, for an extended period. And given what Mungus has just been through..."

Claire felt him tense beneath her hand.

Stillness. Like the bad place. Like the box. Like being trapped.

"No." The word came out before Claire could think about it. "Absolutely not. He just spent twenty-eight days in containment. He flinches when he sees carriers. He sleeps on my chest because he's afraid I'll disappear if he can't feel my heartbeat. I'm not—I can't ask him to—"

"Claire." Martinez's voice was gentle. "I know. I know what he went through, and I know what you went through watching it. But if we don't do something, the alternative is worse. Much worse."

Food lady very upset now. Don't like food lady upset. Makes me upset too.

Outside, the sky flickered briefly—a flash of aurora borealis that shouldn't have been visible in London in daylight. Somewhere in the distance, a car alarm began playing what sounded like Beethoven's Fifth Symphony, the opening notes repeating in an endless loop.

"That's him," Dr. Crumpet said quietly, checking her instruments. "His emotional state is affecting local reality. The more distressed he becomes, the more the dissolution accelerates."

Claire looked down at Mungus, who was pressed against her legs, his fur standing on end, his eyes tracking between the beeping equipment and the strangers in his home. Three days ago, she'd brought him home from containment. Three days ago, she'd promised him he was safe, that no one would ever put him in a box again, that the worst was over.

And now she was going to have to break that promise.

Food lady smells like salt water. Food lady making sad sounds. What is wrong? What did I do wrong?

"You didn't do anything wrong," Claire whispered, scooping him up and holding him against her chest. "This isn't your fault. None of this is your fault."

Then why is food lady crying?

Dr. Ramirez arrived an hour later, carrying a briefcase that hummed with contained starlight. She was a woman in her fifties with calm, competent eyes and hands that moved with the gentle precision of someone who had spent decades treating frightened animals.

Mungus watched her from Claire's lap, his body tense but no longer trembling. The past hour had been spent in quiet preparation—Claire holding him, murmuring reassurances, trying to project a calm she didn't feel. His temperature had stabilized slightly. The aurora effects had stopped flickering quite so erratically. But she could still feel the wrongness in his purr, the rhythm that didn't quite match what it should be.

New person. Smells like herbs and warmth. Moves slowly. Not threatening. But watching.

"Dr. Pemberton," Dr. Ramirez said, extending her hand. Her grip was firm but gentle—the handshake of someone who understood that first impressions mattered, especially with anxious creatures and their equally anxious humans. "I've reviewed the case files. All of them, including the containment records."

"And?"

"And I want you to know that I fought against Mr. Harwick's approach from the beginning. I testified at the preliminary hearing that separation would be counterproductive. I was overruled." Her expression tightened briefly. "What they did to your cat was wrong. I'm sorry you both had to endure it."

Claire felt some of the tension leave her shoulders.

"Thank you. That means a lot."

Vet person fought for me too. Like food lady. Good vet person.

"I should also tell you something about my own history," Dr. Ramirez continued, settling into a chair across from Claire. "Because I think it's relevant to what we're facing today, and I want you to understand why I approach these situations the way I do."

She folded her hands in her lap—a practiced gesture, Claire thought. Something she'd done many times before, preparing to tell a story she'd rather not tell.

"Fifteen years ago, I treated a young gryphon named Artemis. Beautiful creature—golden feathers, the most intelligent eyes you've ever seen. She'd ingested a cursed amulet that her owner's ex-husband had hidden in her food. Deliberate sabotage. The kind of cruelty that still makes me angry when I think about it."

Vet person's voice changed. Talking about sad thing.

"The owner, Margaret, was desperate. The amulet was slowly poisoning Artemis, and we didn't have time for gentle approaches. So I chose surgical intervention. It was faster, more controlled, more predictable. I was confident in my skills. I'd done similar procedures before."

"What happened?"

"The surgery was technically perfect. I removed the amulet without complications. Artemis recovered physically within two weeks." Dr. Ramirez paused. "But she never recovered in the ways that mattered."

Claire's arms tightened around Mungus.

"The trauma of being restrained," Dr. Ramirez continued quietly. "Sedated. Cut open by someone she didn't know, in a place that smelled like fear and antiseptic. She couldn't understand why it was happening. She only knew that she'd been held down against her will, that her body had been violated, that the person she trusted most—Margaret—had allowed it to happen."

Bad things happened to other creature. Creature was scared. Like I was scared.

"Margaret told me, years later, that Artemis would flinch whenever she reached out to pet her. That the gryphon would sleep facing the door, never with her back to the room. That she'd stopped singing—gryphons sing, did you know that?—and never started again." Dr. Ramirez met Claire's eyes. "Artemis lived for another twelve years. But something in her had been broken, and I was the one who broke it."

"That's why you developed the natural approach," Claire said slowly.

"That's why I swore I would never again choose efficiency over trust. Never again prioritize my timeline over the creature's consent." Dr. Ramirez leaned forward. "The procedure I'm proposing today is slower than surgery. It's less predictable. It requires active cooperation from Mungus in a way that surgical intervention wouldn't. But it works *with* him instead of against him."

Vet person learned from bad thing. Trying to do better thing now.

"What does cooperation mean, exactly?" Claire asked. "Agent Martinez mentioned stillness. Physical restraint."

"Not restraint. That's the crucial distinction." Dr. Ramirez's voice was firm. "I don't need anyone to hold Mungus down. I need him to choose to be still. To let you hold him—not because he's trapped, but because he trusts that you're keeping him safe."

"And if he can't do that? If the trauma from containment is too fresh?"

"Then we don't proceed. I won't force this. I *can't* force this—the procedure requires genuine consent, genuine calm. Any struggling, any panic, and the mystical components won't work properly. The artifact could destabilize violently instead of expelling safely."

Don't understand all the words. Understand vet person is different from bad place people.

Dr. Ramirez stood and moved slowly toward Claire and Mungus, telegraphing every motion. She crouched down a few feet away, making herself small, non-threatening.

"Hello, Mungus," she said softly. "I know you've been through something terrible. I know strangers haven't been kind to you recently. I'm not going to touch you unless you want me to. I just wanted to introduce myself."

New person talking to me directly. Not over my head. Respecting me.

Mungus studied her for a long moment. Then, cautiously, he extended his nose toward her outstretched hand.

Smells like... calm. Like someone who knows how to wait.

"Good boy," Dr. Ramirez murmured. "Good, brave boy."

They talked for another hour. Dr. Ramirez explained the procedure in detail—the mystical preparations, the biological triggers, the expected sequence of events. She answered every question Claire asked, and several that Claire hadn't thought to ask. She never once suggested that time was running out, that they needed to hurry, that Claire's concerns were less important than the cosmic emergency unfolding in her cat's digestive system.

But the emergency was unfolding. Claire could see it in the way Mungus's aurora effects kept stuttering, in the growing warmth of his fur, in the moments—brief but unmistakable—when parts of him became slightly transparent.

Stomach hurts more now. Strange thing getting stranger.

"I need to talk to him," Claire said finally. "Alone. Before I can ask him to do this."

Dr. Ramirez nodded as if she'd been expecting this. "Take all the time you need. We'll be in the other room."

When they'd gone, Claire carried Mungus to the couch and sat with him in her lap, facing the window. The afternoon light was golden, peaceful, completely at odds with the crisis unfolding inside both of them.

Just food lady and me now. Better. Safer.

"I need to tell you something," Claire said, her voice barely above a whisper. "And I need you to really listen, okay? Not just hear my sounds, but understand what I'm trying to say."

Listening. Always listening to food lady.

She took a deep breath. This was the hardest thing she'd ever had to do. Harder than defending him at the committee. Harder than watching them carry him away. Because this time, she was the one asking him to be afraid.

"Remember when you ate that weird glowing thing? The one that tasted like chicken but felt like forever?"

Yes. Crunchy thing. Strange aftertaste. Seemed like good idea at the time.

"It's still inside you. And it's dissolving. That's why you've been feeling strange—why you keep flickering, why your purr doesn't sound right. The thing you ate is falling apart, and if we don't get it out, it's going to cause problems. Not just for reality—for you. You might get very sick. You might change into something different. Something that doesn't remember being my cat anymore."

Don't want to change. Don't want to forget food lady.

"Dr. Ramirez thinks she can help you throw it up. Like a really big hairball. But the procedure—" Claire's voice caught. "The procedure needs you to stay very still. Completely still, for a while. And I'd have to hold you."

She felt him tense in her arms.

Holding. Like the bad box. Scared.

"Not like the bad place," Claire said quickly. "Not in a box, not restrained by strangers. Just me. Holding you. While Dr. Ramirez does her thing."

But... still can't move. Still trapped.

"I know." Her voice broke. "I know what I'm asking. I know you just got home. I know you're scared of anything that feels like containment. I know you sleep on my chest because you're afraid I'll disappear if you can't feel my heartbeat."

Food lady understands. Food lady always understands.

"And I know I promised you that the worst was over. That you were safe. That no one would ever put you in a box again." Tears were sliding down her face now, dripping onto his fur. "I'm so sorry. I'm so sorry I have to ask you this. If there was any other way—"

Food lady crying. Don't like food lady crying. Makes my chest hurt worse than stomach.

Mungus pulled back to look at her face. His eyes were glowing more than usual—golden-green with flecks of starlight—and in them, Claire saw something she hadn't expected.

Not fear. Not confusion.

Understanding.

Food lady asking. Not demanding. Not forcing. Asking.

"If you don't want to do this," Claire whispered, "we'll figure out something else. I don't care if reality gets weird. I don't care if the Thames flows uphill or gravity becomes optional. I will not ask you to be afraid again unless you're willing. Do you understand? This is your choice. Your choice, not mine."

Food lady asking. Not making me.

Mungus stared at her for a long moment, the choice settling in the space between them. In the bad place, they had taken him. Here, she was asking.

Then, slowly, deliberately, he climbed fully into her lap and went limp.

Trust food lady. Always trust food lady.

"Are you sure?" Claire's voice was barely audible. "Mungus, are you sure? Because once we start—"

He pressed his forehead against her chin, a gesture of pure, unconditional trust. Sure.

Claire gathered him close, pressing her face into his fur, feeling his warmth and his weight and his impossible, unearned, freely-given trust.

"Okay," she whispered. "Okay. We'll do this together."

Outside, the sky had begun to glow with colors that

shouldn't exist in a London afternoon. Somewhere across the city, in a containment facility he would never see again, a cosmic alarm clock noted the shift in its readings and quietly revised its projections.

Claire's arms tightened around him.

"Okay," she whispered. "Okay. We'll do this together."

Together. Yes. That is the only way.

8
THE GREAT REGURGITATION PROTOCOL

"Courage isn't the absence of fear. Courage is a cat eating diet tuna because someone he loves asked him to."

The kitchen had been transformed.

Harold had arrived while Claire and Mungus were having their conversation, and he'd brought what he described as "emergency feng shui supplies"—crystals, candles, small brass bowls arranged in geometric patterns that made Claire's eyes water slightly if she looked at them too long.

"The spatial arrangement matters enormously," Harold explained, adjusting a candle by precisely two millimeters. "Mystical procedures require proper aesthetic harmony. I've cross-referenced seven different traditions and filed the specifications under 'Optimal Mystical-Veterinary Spatial Configurations.' It's a new category. I'm very excited about it."

Forms creature made things nice. Looks like important ceremony space. Smells like good intentions.

Dr. Ramirez surveyed the setup with evident approval. "This is genuinely impressive work, Harold. The energy flow is excellent."

"Thank you." Harold practically glowed. "I've also prepared preliminary documentation for all potential outcomes, including Form 47-B: Successful Artifact Expulsion, Form 47-C: Partial Artifact Expulsion Requiring Follow-Up, and Form 47-D: Catastrophic Reality Destabilization. Just in case."

"Let's aim for 47-B," Martinez said dryly.

"Oh, absolutely. But proper preparation means planning for all contingencies." Harold patted his stack of forms lovingly. "These are ready for anything."

Forms creature very prepared. Good to have prepared creatures nearby.

Claire stood in the doorway, Mungus still cradled against her chest. He'd been calm since his decision—calmer than she'd expected, actually. His purr had steadied into something that almost sounded normal, and his aurora effects had settled into gentle, rhythmic pulses.

Made choice. Committed to choice. Now just need to do the thing.

"Are you ready?" Dr. Ramirez asked softly.

Claire looked down at Mungus. He looked up at her.

Ready. Scared, but ready. Food lady is here. Everything else is manageable.

"We're ready," Claire said.

Dr. Ramirez prepared the mystical components with the careful precision of someone who had done this many times before. Each element was handled with respect, placed with intention, arranged in patterns that Claire didn't understand but could somehow feel the rightness of.

The liquid moonlight shimmered in its crystal bottle, casting silver patterns across the ceiling. The herbs—dried lavender, something that smelled like distant summers, a sprig of something Claire didn't recognize but that made Mungus's nose twitch with interest—were arranged in a small brass bowl. And the Phoenix feather, secured in its containment unit, radiated a warmth that seemed to seep into the air itself.

"The first phase prepares his system," Dr. Ramirez explained, mixing the components with a glass stirring rod that seemed to bend light around itself. "The moonlight soothes cosmic energy. The herbs relax the physical body. The Phoenix essence provides a template for transformation—a reminder that things can be released and renewed without being destroyed."

Interesting smells. Good smells. Like safe things and warm places.

She poured the mixture into a silver bowl and set it in front of Mungus, who had been placed on a cushion in the center of Harold's geometric arrangement.

"This part he can do on his own," Dr. Ramirez said. "No holding required yet. Let him approach it at his own pace."

Bowl smells very good. Like the best nap. Like food lady's lap after a long day.

Mungus sniffed the mixture cautiously, then looked up at Claire.

"It's okay," she assured him. "Dr. Ramirez made it to help you."

Food lady says safe. Will try.

He lapped at the mixture tentatively at first, then with increasing enthusiasm as the flavors registered.

Excellent. Complex notes of starlight and distant summer. Like eating a good dream.

His purr deepened as warmth spread through his system. The aurora effects around him brightened, cycling through colors that seemed healthier somehow—less erratic, more harmonious.

"Good," Dr. Ramirez murmured, watching her monitoring devices. "Very good. His energy is settling. The preparation is integrating properly."

Feel warm. Feel calm. Feel like everything might actually be okay.

"Phase two," Dr. Ramirez announced. She reached into her case and produced a small can that seemed to radiate disappointment even before she opened it.

That smell. Know that smell. No. No no no.

Mungus's purr stopped abruptly. His ears flattened against his skull, and his tail puffed to approximately twice its normal size.

DIET TUNA. THE ABOMINATION. THE FAKE FISH. THE PHILOSOPHICAL BETRAYAL IN EDIBLE FORM.

"I know," Claire said, recognizing his reaction with a mixture of sympathy and—she couldn't help it—slight amusement. "I know it's awful."

IT IS NOT JUST AWFUL. IT IS A CRIME AGAINST THE VERY CONCEPT OF TUNA. IT CLAIMS TO BE FISH. IT IS NOT FISH. IT IS LIES IN A CAN.

"Dr. Ramirez says the disgust response will help trigger the regurgitation. Your body will want to reject it, and when it does, the artifact should come up too."

COULD TRIGGER REGURGITATION WITH DIGNITY. COULD EAT SOMETHING ACTUALLY DISGUSTING. A HAIRBALL. A PIECE OF THAT PLASTIC THING FOOD LADY DROPPED LAST WEEK. ANYTHING BUT THE DIET TUNA.

"The cognitive dissonance is the key," Dr. Ramirez explained, watching Mungus's escalating distress with professional interest. "He expects tuna. He gets something that betrays every expectation of what tuna should be. The violation is so profound that his entire system rebels against it."

"He really, really hates diet tuna," Claire warned.

"Good. The stronger the aversion, the more effective the trigger."

FOOD LADY. PLEASE. WE HAVE DISCUSSED THIS. WE AGREED NEVER AGAIN.

Claire knelt down beside him, her heart aching at his obvious distress. But she could also see the transparency flickering at the edges of his ears again, could feel the wrongness in his cosmic signature even without Dr. Crumpet's instruments.

"Hey," she said softly. "Remember what I asked you? About trusting me?"

Remember. Made choice. Chose to trust.

"This is the hard part. The part where trust actually costs something. I know the diet tuna is horrible. I know you hate it more than anything. But I need you to eat it, and then I need you to let me hold you still while your body processes the rejection."

But... but it's DIET TUNA.

"I know, baby. I know."

She reached for the can, and the smell hit her immediately—that particular combination of fish and chemicals and disappointment that somehow managed to be offensive even to human noses. She understood, suddenly, why this would work. The diet tuna wasn't just bad food. It was a betrayal of the very concept of food.

For food lady. Must do scary thing. Eat the bad tuna.

Mungus approached the bowl with the dignity of someone walking toward their own execution. He stared at the diet tuna for a long moment—seventeen seconds, Claire counted, each one feeling like an hour.

Then he consumed it in a single, decisive gulp.

And immediately backed into Claire's arms, going rigid with revulsion.

HORRIBLE. FAKE. WRONG. EVERYTHING ABOUT IT WRONG. BETRAYAL. LIES. THE WORST TASTE IN THE HISTORY OF TASTING.

"I've got you," Claire whispered, wrapping her arms around him. "I've got you. This is nothing like the bad place. I'm right here. I'm not letting go."

Food lady's arms. Not cold box. Not alone. Food lady's arms.

"He needs to stay calm," Dr. Ramirez said, watching her monitors. "The mystical preparation is activating, but if he panics, the rejection could become violent rather than controlled."

"He won't panic," Claire said. She could feel him trembling against her chest, could feel his revulsion at what he'd just swallowed. But underneath the physical disgust, she could also feel his trust—solid, steady, anchoring him even through the discomfort.

Trust food lady. Trust food lady. Stomach feels VERY STRANGE now.

Strange thing inside waking up. Wants out. Diet tuna making everything want out.

The regurgitation began.

It started with what Dr. Ramirez later described as "textbook form"—a series of increasingly intense contractions that Claire could feel rippling through Mungus's small body. She held him steady, keeping her breathing slow and even, trying to project a calm she didn't entirely feel.

Strange. Very strange. Things moving inside. Things that shouldn't be there.

The artifact emerged first.

It was no longer the crystalline structure Claire remembered from the night everything began. The Seal of Final Things had transformed during its months inside Mungus—compressed, digested, reconstituted into something that had become a snow globe containing a small, perfectly normal Tuesday.

The globe landed with a gentle thump on Harold's carefully arranged geometric pattern and immediately began humming show tunes.

Round thing out. Good. Feels better already. But... more coming.

More came.

Claire's missing thesis chapter emerged next, wrapped in cosmic mucus but otherwise intact. Dr. Crumpet grabbed it before it could touch the floor, her eyes wide with academic excitement.

"The citations have been enhanced," she breathed. "These references don't exist in any known library. This could revolutionize the field."

Food lady's paper thing. Was worried about that. Glad it came back.

A small pile of items followed—keys that didn't match any known locks, socks that had been lost in parallel dimensions, a postcard from somewhere that looked like London but had three moons in the sky. The Dimension of Mild Inconvenience was apparently surrendering its treasures.

Then came something else.

Something that glowed.

"That," Dr. Crumpet said, her voice suddenly sharp, "is not supposed to be here."

Glowing ball. Tuesday smell. Very strong Tuesday smell. Not supposed to be outside.

The orb was about the size of a tennis ball when it emerged, perfectly spherical, containing what appeared to be an entire day compressed into a space smaller than Mungus's food bowl. Through its translucent surface, Claire could see fragments of time playing out in miniature—morning commuters, afternoon tea, evening news broadcasts, all layered on top of each other in an impossible temporal collage.

"Is that—" Claire started.

"Last Tuesday," Dr. Crumpet confirmed. "The one that went missing during his containment. It must have gotten caught in the artifact's dissolution process."

Ate a Tuesday? Don't remember eating a Tuesday.

"It was probably absorbed during one of his stress episodes," Dr. Ramirez said, her voice carefully controlled. "Cosmic cats under extreme duress can accidentally consume nearby temporal fragments. It's rare, but documented."

"Is it dangerous?"

The orb answered the question by beginning to expand.

It grew slowly at first—tennis ball to softball, softball to grapefruit. Claire could feel Mungus tensing in her arms, could feel his instinct to run, to escape the strange glowing thing that was getting bigger in the middle of his kitchen.

Big now. Getting bigger. Don't like it.

"Keep holding him," Dr. Ramirez commanded. "His calm is the only thing keeping this from accelerating."

"What happens if it accelerates?"

"If that Tuesday fully decompresses in this space—" Dr. Crumpet was pulling devices from her bag, instruments that beeped and whirred and glowed with urgent warning lights. "We'd have temporal overlap. Two days trying to exist in the same physical location. Reality doesn't handle contradictions well. It gets... creative."

Bigger. Much bigger now. Beach ball sized. People inside.

Through the expanding surface, Claire could see details

resolving—the morning commute in miniature, a woman reaching for a coffee cup she would never quite grasp, the 9:15 train to King's Cross eternally approaching a platform it would never reach.

"Everyone step back," Dr. Ramirez ordered. "Everyone except Claire. Mungus's field is the only thing keeping this contained."

Me? Keeping it contained? But I'm scared.

"You're doing it," Claire whispered to him. "Your purr is stabilizing the temporal field. Can you feel it? Your calm is holding everything together."

Purr feels different. Heavier. Like it's carrying something.

The orb shuddered. Inside, the compressed Tuesday seemed to ripple, and for a moment the people frozen inside flickered with awareness—commuters suddenly uncertain why they couldn't move, why time had stopped, why everything felt wrong.

"They're waking up," Dr. Crumpet said urgently. "If they become fully conscious inside the compression—"

"Harold!" Martinez shouted. "Form 47-Q: Emergency Temporal Containment. Now!"

"I have three copies prepared!" Harold's voice was high with a mixture of excitement and terror. "All subclauses included! The Department of Temporal Affairs has been notified!"

Forms creature helping. Everyone trying to help. Just need to stay calm. Calm calm calm.

The orb had grown to the size of a small child now. Inside, the woman with the coffee cup made a sound—not quite a word, but something that suggested confusion, desperation, a growing awareness that something was terribly wrong with the shape of time around her.

"Claire," Dr. Ramirez said urgently. "His readings are fluctuating. If he panics—"

"He won't panic." Claire tightened her arms around Mungus, feeling his small body rigid with effort. "Look at me," she told him. "Not at the scary thing. Look at me."

Food lady's eyes. Looking at food lady's eyes.

"Remember when you ate that entire rotisserie chicken while my old housemates dealt with the kitchen fire? Remember how focused you were? Nothing could distract you from that chicken."

Good chicken. Very good chicken. Maximum focus chicken.

"I need you to be that focused now. Not on the scary thing. On us. On staying calm. On trusting that we're going to get through this together."

Calm. Calm like chicken. Calm like food lady's heartbeat.

His purr, which had been stuttering and irregular, began to find its rhythm. Claire felt the vibration spreading through her chest, felt it finding a pattern, felt it reaching out to touch the chaos around them.

Can do this. Food lady believes in me. Can do this.

The orb's expansion slowed. Inside, the frozen commuters stilled, their brief moment of awareness fading back into temporal suspension.

"It's working," Dr. Crumpet breathed. "He's actually stabilizing it."

"But we can't hold this forever," Dr. Ramirez said. "We need to contain it properly before he exhausts himself. Martinez—"

Agent Martinez was already moving, setting crystals at regular intervals around a ritual circle of salt and silver. Her hands were steady, but Claire could see sweat on her forehead. This wasn't in any manual. This wasn't a crisis anyone had trained for.

"The chamber," Dr. Ramirez said, maneuvering a device resembling a cross between a birdcage and a snow globe into position. "I need to get this around the orb before it expands past the opening. If I time it wrong—"

"Don't time it wrong," Martinez said grimly.

Tuesday ball still growing. But slower now. Purr holding. Calm holding. Food lady holding.

"You're extraordinary," Claire whispered to Mungus. "You're holding reality together with your purr. How many cats can say that?"

Am special cat. Food lady is right.

"Almost there," Dr. Ramirez murmured, inching the containment chamber into position. The orb was pressing against its crystalline walls now, temporal energy crackling against mystical boundaries. "Just need to—"

The chamber clicked into place.

The symbols etched into its surface flared brilliant gold. Claire felt a pressure in her ears—not quite sound, something adjacent to sound, something that existed in the spaces between moments.

And the Tuesday's expansion stopped.

Inside the crystal cage, the compressed day settled into something that looked almost peaceful. The commuters froze in their eternal loops, but they no longer seemed distressed. The woman finally grasped her coffee cup, and though she would never drink it, at least she held it.

Tuesday ball contained. Did it. We did it.

The silence that followed was the most beautiful sound Claire had ever heard.

Three Hours Later

The kitchen had been mostly restored to normal—aside from the crystal-caged Tuesday sitting in the corner like the world's strangest snow globe, and the enhanced thesis chapter that Dr. Crumpet had already begun analyzing with academic fervor.

"The citations reference journals that won't be founded for another fifty years," she was murmuring to herself. "This is going to require a whole new approach to temporal bibliography..."

Scientists finding interesting things. Good. Like when food lady gets excited about book things.

Mungus had been thoroughly examined by Dr. Ramirez, who pronounced him "cosmically stable and remarkably healthy, considering." His temperature had returned to normal. His purr had regained its proper rhythm. And the transparency that had been flickering at his edges had resolved completely.

"The artifact is gone," Dr. Ramirez confirmed. "Fully expelled. His system is integrating the residual cosmic energy naturally now, without the destabilizing influence of the Seal. He's still significant, but in a sustainable way."

Feel better. Much better. Stomach empty of strange things. Only regular food from now on.

No more glowing objects. No more diet tuna. No more Tuesdays.

Claire hadn't let go of him since the containment. She held him in her lap now, running her hands through his fur, unable to stop checking that he was solid, that he was real, that the crisis was actually over.

"The bond between you has actually strengthened," Dr. Ramirez added, gathering her equipment. "The trust required for the procedure created a deeper connection than existed before. His cosmic signature is more stable now than it's been since he ate the artifact in the first place."

"So he's going to be okay?"

"Better than okay. He's going to be exactly what you always hoped—a cat with unusual abilities and a very strong attachment to his human. The cosmic significance stays. The instability goes."

Stay with food lady. Have interesting powers. Make good things happen. Perfect arrangement.

Agent Martinez approached as the others packed up. Her professional mask had slipped; she looked tired but genuinely happy.

"You know what this means for the Ministry?" she said. "Complete validation of everything we argued for. Harwick's containment made things worse. Your bond made things better. It's all documented, all official, all ready to become policy."

"Good," Claire said, her voice steady. "I want it on record. I want it in every file, every report, every future case study. When someone's cosmic pet gets sick, I want the first thing they read to be: 'Love and trust are not weaknesses to be managed. They are strengths to be supported.'"

Good words. Important words. Other cosmic creatures should know.

"I'll make sure Harold gets that exact wording into the official documentation," Martinez promised.

From his workstation, Harold looked up with shining eyes. "That's going to require a new form category. 'Documentation of Emotional Factors in Cosmic Entity Management.' Form EF-1 through EF-12, with subcategories for different bond types and enhancement levels." He clutched his typewriter with visible emotion. "It's going to be beautiful."

Claire laughed—the first real laugh since the crisis began, free and full and relieved.

"Make it beautiful, Harold. Make it the most beautiful forms you've ever designed."

That Night

The flat was quiet.

Everyone had finally left—Dr. Ramirez to her clinic, Dr. Crumpet to her temporal research, Martinez to file preliminary reports, Harold to begin designing his new form categories with what he'd described as "unprecedented enthusiasm."

Claire sat on her couch with Mungus in her lap, watching the aurora effects dance gently across her ceiling. The compressed Tuesday glowed softly in its cage on the kitchen counter, humming a lullaby now instead of show tunes, as if it too had found peace.

Good quiet. Safe quiet. Home quiet.

"I'm proud of you," Claire said softly. "You did something impossible today. You ate diet tuna."

Do not mention the diet tuna. Am trying to forget the diet tuna.

"You stayed calm when a whole Tuesday was expanding in the kitchen."

That was very concerning. Glad it is in cage now.

"You trusted me. Even after everything that happened. Even after I had to ask you to do something that scared you."

Trust is not question. Trust is foundation.

He pressed his forehead against her chin—his favorite gesture, the one that meant love and safety and home all at once.

Food lady fought for me. Food lady came for me. Food lady asked me to be brave, and I was brave, and now scary thing is over and we are together.

This is how it should be. This is how it always should be.

"Always," Claire agreed, her voice thick with tears that weren't sadness anymore. "You and me. Together. Always."

Outside, the stars were coming out—slightly brighter than usual, as if the universe was celebrating. The cosmic alarm clock that had been tracking the end of the world updated its calculations, found them unexpectedly optimistic, and settled into a gentle hum of satisfaction.

Tomorrow would bring new challenges—forms to file, reports to write, a whole Ministry to help establish. But tonight, there was just this: a woman and her cat, a crisis survived, a bond strengthened.

Good night. Hard day. But good ending.

On the kitchen counter, the compressed Tuesday shifted in its crystal cage and began humming something that sounded almost like a lullaby. Mungus's ears twitched toward it, then settled.

Acceptable music. Will allow.

His purr deepened, harmonizing briefly with the trapped day's song, and Claire felt the vibration spread through her chest like warmth, like safety, like home.

9
THE NEW DEPARTMENT OF MOSTLY SATISFACTORY ENDINGS

"The best solutions are the ones that make everyone slightly confused but generally content, which is the highest form of success any government department can hope to achieve."

Three Weeks After the Great Regurgitation Protocol

The Ministry of Unusual Pet Incidents and Related Concerns occupied the third floor of a converted Victorian building in South Kensington, sandwiched between the Department of Temporal Affairs and an Office of Reasonable Impossibilities that no one would explain.

Claire stood in the doorway of her new office, trying to process that she had an office. With a window. And a nameplate that read "Dr. Claire Pemberton, Chief Cat Liaison" in letters that occasionally shimmered with cosmic significance.

New den. Smells like fresh paint and old paper. Acceptable.

Mungus had already claimed the sunny spot beneath the

window, where a custom cat bed had been installed at taxpayer expense. The bed featured temperature-regulating fabric that seemed to anticipate his preferences, a small built-in fountain, and what Harold had described as "optimal feng shui positioning for cosmic energy flow."

"It's better than my bed at home," Claire observed.

Good bed. Food lady can visit here.

Agent Martinez appeared in the doorway with a stack of folders and a smile. "Welcome to your first official day. Ready to learn how much paperwork cosmic cat management actually involves?"

"I survived three years of graduate school. I can handle paperwork."

"That's what they all say." Martinez set the folders on Claire's desk with a thump that suggested she wasn't joking. "These are the outstanding incident reports from the past month. Most are Level 1—Beneficial Cosmic Events that just need documentation. A few Level 2s that need follow-up. And one Level 3 that we're monitoring."

"What's the Level 3?"

"A family in Bristol whose daughter's hamster appears to have developed prophetic abilities after eating a piece of meteorite. It keeps predicting minor inconveniences—traffic jams, delayed trains, that sort of thing. Very accurate, but the family's not sure what to do with the information."

Hamster with prophecy. Unusual. Would investigate.

Claire felt a laugh bubbling up. "A prophetic hamster. Of course."

"Welcome to the Ministry." Martinez's eyes crinkled. "The strangest part is how quickly this all starts to feel normal. Give it a month, and you'll be filing reports about reality fluctuations like it's the most natural thing in the world."

Strange things feel normal now.

"I'm already halfway there," Claire admitted. "This morning, Mungus sneezed and the weather changed. I just made a note for the report and finished my coffee."

"Perfect. You're going to fit in just fine."

The Prophetic Hamster Incident

Two weeks into her tenure, Claire faced her first real crisis.

"The hamster situation in Bristol has escalated," Martinez announced, appearing in Claire's office doorway with a tablet showing news footage of a small crowd gathered outside a suburban house. "The family posted a video of Nutmeg predicting a minor earthquake. It went viral. Now there are people camped outside their home demanding prophecies."

Hamster causing problems. Should have investigated when had chance.

Claire looked up from the report she'd been reading. "How viral?"

"Two million views and counting. The hashtag #PropheticHamster is trending in twelve countries. The family is overwhelmed, the hamster is stressed, and the predictions are getting more erratic. This morning Nutmeg apparently predicted both sunshine and apocalyptic flooding for the same afternoon."

"That's not how prophecy works," Claire said slowly.

"Is it?"

"Dr. Crumpet says contradictory predictions are a sign of entity distress. When a cosmically significant being is overwhelmed, their abilities become unreliable." Martinez set the tablet down. "The family is asking for help. Officially. Through proper channels. Form CS-7: Request for Ministry Intervention in Escalating Cosmic Pet Situation."

Claire felt a flicker of the old anxiety—the voice that said she wasn't qualified for this, that she was just a graduate student who'd gotten lucky, that someone more experienced should handle it. But then she looked at Mungus, who was watching her from his temperature-regulated cat bed with an expression of complete confidence.

Food lady knows what to do. Food lady always knows.

"Okay," Claire said, standing up. "What do we know about the family?"

"Parents, two kids, the hamster belonged to the daughter originally. They've had Nutmeg for three years. No previous cosmic incidents. The meteorite fragment was a birthday gift from an uncle who collects 'interesting rocks.'" Martinez consulted her tablet. "The uncle has been contacted. He had no idea the rock was significant. He bought it at a car boot sale in Devon."

"Of course he did." Claire grabbed her jacket. "And the hamster's bond with the daughter—is it strong? Documented?"

"According to the intake form, the daughter, Emily, age nine, considers Nutmeg her best friend. She's been sleeping next to the cage every night since the crowds started gathering. She's terrified someone is going to take him away."

Small human protecting small creature. Understands importance of bond.

Claire felt something click into place. She knew this situation. She'd lived this situation.

"I know what to do," she said. "We need to get the crowds away from the house, give the family some space, and help Emily understand that she's not losing her hamster. The predictions are erratic because Nutmeg is scared. Once he feels safe again, his abilities should stabilize."

"You think it's that simple?"

"I think cosmic entities aren't that different from regular pets. They need safety, routine, and the people they love." Claire headed for the door, then paused. "And maybe we should bring Mungus. If proximity to a stabilized cosmic cat helped Mr. Whiskers develop his abilities, maybe it can help calm an overstressed prophetic hamster."

Will help small prophecy creature. Am expert in being cosmic pet.

Martinez smiled. "I'll arrange transport. And Claire?"

"Yes?"

"This is exactly what you were hired for. You're going to do great."

She was reviewing Form CE-4 (Cosmic Entity Dietary Preferences, Monthly Update) when a knock at her door made her look up.

Gerald Harwick stood in the doorway.

Hostile person. Here. In our den.

Mungus's fur rose slightly, but Claire put a hand on him before his cosmic field could react. "Mr. Harwick."

He looked different. Smaller, somehow—not physically, but in the way he occupied space. The sharp confidence that had dominated the committee room was gone. He wore the same precise suit, carried the same leather portfolio, but something fundamental had shifted.

"Dr. Pemberton." He didn't enter the office. "I was reassigned to this building last week. Interdepartmental Liaison for Fiscal Oversight." His mouth twisted slightly. "It's three floors down. Considerably less... significant."

"I'm sorry to hear that," Claire said, and was surprised to find she meant it. Not sorry he'd lost power—sorry that anyone had to feel diminished.

"Are you?" He studied her face. "I would have thought you'd be pleased."

Don't like hostile person. But hostile person smells different now. Smells like confusion.

"I'm not pleased when anyone suffers. That was rather the point of everything I argued for."

Harwick was quiet for a moment. Then: "I've been trying to understand where I went wrong. The data supported containment. The risk assessment was sound. The fiscal projections were accurate."

"The fiscal projections were accurate," Claire agreed. "The fish showers alone cost more than my annual budget."

"Because containment made things worse. I know. I've read the reports." He shifted his weight, uncomfortable. "What I don't understand is *why*. Why would separating an unstable entity from its emotional attachment increase instability? It's counterintuitive."

Claire looked at Mungus, who was watching Harwick with wary attention.

"It's only counterintuitive if you think of bonds as weaknesses," she said slowly. "As variables that cloud judgment and complicate management. But bonds aren't weaknesses, Mr. Harwick. They're load-bearing structures. Remove them and the whole building comes down."

Food lady explaining important things. Hostile person listening. Strange.

Harwick frowned. "That's not how systems work. Redundancy requires independence. If one component fails—"

"Mungus isn't a component. He's a being. With feelings and preferences and relationships that matter to him." Claire met Harwick's eyes. "You kept asking whether love was a sufficient basis for managing a cosmic entity. The answer is yes. It's the only sufficient basis. Everything else is just paperwork."

The silence stretched between them. Harwick's expression cycled through something complicated—resistance, confusion, and finally something that might have been the first crack in a very old wall.

"I don't understand that," he said finally. "I'm not sure I'm capable of understanding it."

"That's honest, at least."

Hostile person being honest. Did not expect.

He nodded once, stiffly, and turned to leave. At the door, he paused.

"For what it's worth, Dr. Pemberton, I didn't want to hurt your cat. I genuinely believed I was protecting the public."

"I know," Claire said. "That's what made you so dangerous."

He left without responding. But Claire noticed that he walked differently than he had in the committee room—less like someone who had all the answers, more like someone who had just discovered he might have been asking the wrong questions.

Hostile person gone. Good. But... different hostile person than before.

Not angry smell now. Smells... sad. And small.

Bristol

The Hartley family's home was surrounded by a crowd of approximately fifty people when Claire arrived, ranging from earnest believers seeking guidance to skeptical journalists to one woman holding a sign that read "NUTMEG FOR PRIME MINISTER."

Many stressed humans. Stressed hamster inside. Bad situation.

"Dr. Pemberton?" A man emerged from the crowd—Mr. Hartley, Claire presumed, looking exhausted and overwhelmed. "Thank God you're here. We didn't know who else to call."

"I'm Chief Cat Liaison for the Ministry of Unusual Pet Incidents," Claire said, pulling out her badge with practiced efficiency. "We have protocols for this situation. Form CS-7 has been filed, and we'll be implementing Standard Containment Procedure Alpha for—"

She stopped.

Mr. Hartley's face had gone pale. Behind him, Mrs. Hartley had appeared in the doorway, and her expression was worse—the particular terror of someone who had just heard the word "containment" and understood exactly what it might mean.

Food lady using wrong words. Scared people more.

"No," Mrs. Hartley said, her voice shaking. "No, you're not taking him. Emily won't survive it. She's barely sleeping as it is, and if you people come in here with your forms and your procedures and your—"

"That's not—" Claire started, but she could hear herself, hear the bureaucratic distance in her own voice, and suddenly she was back in her own kitchen, facing Agent Martinez for the first time, hearing words like "unauthorized cosmic entity" and "containment protocols" and feeling her world collapse.

She had become the thing she'd fought against.

Food lady realizing something. Important realization.

"I'm sorry," Claire said. She put the badge away. "I started wrong. Can I try again?"

The Hartleys exchanged uncertain glances.

"Please," Claire said. "I know what you're going through. Not professionally—personally. A few months ago, people came to my home with forms and protocols and took my cat away. I spent twenty-eight days fighting to get him back."

Mrs. Hartley's expression shifted slightly. "You're the Doomsday Cat woman. I saw you on the news."

"His name is Mungus." Claire held up his carrier. "And he's here to help. Not to contain anyone or fill out forms or implement procedures. Just to help."

Good. Food lady using better words now.

The tension didn't disappear, but it eased. Mr. Hartley's shoulders dropped slightly. Mrs. Hartley stepped back from the doorway.

"Emily won't stop crying," Mrs. Hartley said quietly. "She thinks you're here to take Nutmeg away. She's been sleeping next to his cage every night, like she can protect him just by being there."

Claire felt her throat tighten. "Can I talk to her? Just talk. No forms, no protocols. Just one person who loves a cosmic pet talking to another."

A long pause. Then Mrs. Hartley nodded.

Good. Food lady fixed mistake. Now can help.

Emily Hartley was nine years old, with red-rimmed eyes and a hamster cage clutched protectively in her arms. Inside the cage, a small golden hamster was running frantically on his wheel, occasionally stopping to squeak in patterns that might have been prophetic but mostly sounded panicked.

"They want to take him," Emily said immediately, her voice thick with tears. "The people outside. And now you. Everyone wants to take Nutmeg away."

Claire didn't approach. She sat down on the floor, making herself small, making herself unthreatening. Mungus, understanding the assignment, settled into her lap and began to purr softly.

"I'm not here to take him," Claire said. "I'm here because I know exactly how you feel."

"You don't know."

"I do." Claire kept her voice gentle. "A few months ago, some people decided my cat was too important to live with me. They said he'd be safer with professionals. They put him in a special cage and took him away, and I didn't see him for almost a month."

Emily's grip on the hamster cage loosened slightly. "What happened?"

"I fought for him. Every single day. And eventually, I won." Claire met Emily's eyes. "I'm here to make sure you don't have to fight like I did. To make sure nobody takes Nutmeg away from you."

Small human listening now. Fear-smell getting less.

"Really?"

"Really. But I need you to understand something first." Claire leaned forward slightly. "The reason I won—the reason Mungus got to come home—is because the people making decisions finally understood that our bond was the most important thing. Not procedures. Not containment. The love between us."

Inside the cage, Nutmeg had stopped his frantic running. He was watching Mungus now, whiskers twitching.

"The same is true for you and Nutmeg," Claire continued. "His abilities got weird because he's scared. Because there are strangers outside and his person is frightened and everything feels wrong. But you're his anchor, Emily. Your love is what keeps him stable."

"My love?"

"Your love." Claire smiled. "Can I show you something?"

She held Mungus closer to the hamster cage. Mungus, understanding perfectly, began to purr—not his reality-warping purr, but something softer. A purr designed to soothe.

Safe now. Our humans are here.

Nutmeg stopped twitching. His tiny body relaxed. He sat

very still, looking at Mungus with something that might have been recognition.

You understand. Good. We protect each other by protecting them.

"He looks better," Emily whispered.

"He feels better. Because you're here, and you're protecting him, and now he knows there are other people who understand."

Emily looked at Claire with new eyes. "You almost messed up, didn't you? When you got here. You were being all official and scary."

Small human noticed. Small human smart.

Claire laughed, surprised by the girl's directness. "Yes. I almost messed up badly. I forgot what it felt like to be on your side of things."

"But then you remembered."

"Then I remembered." Claire stood, brushing off her knees. "That's something I have to keep remembering, actually. It's easy to become the thing you fought against if you're not careful."

Important lesson. Food lady still learning. Good.

Emily set down the hamster cage for the first time since Claire had arrived. Inside, Nutmeg had curled into a small, peaceful ball.

"You're different than I expected," Emily said. "The Ministry people, I mean. I thought you'd be all forms and rules."

"There are forms and rules," Claire admitted. "My friend Harold is going to help your parents fill out paperwork that officially protects Nutmeg as a registered cosmic entity. But the forms aren't the point. They're just tools to make sure the point is protected."

"What's the point?"

Claire looked at Mungus, then at Nutmeg, then at Emily.

"That love matters. That bonds matter. That sometimes the most important thing a government can do is get out of the way and let people take care of each other."

Good words. Best words. Food lady remembering important things now.

The Friendship of Cosmic Cat Owners

Wednesday evenings had become sacred.

It had started as professional check-ins—Agent Martinez stopping by Claire's flat to review the week's reports, discuss upcoming incidents, make sure Mungus's cosmic readings remained stable. But somewhere along the way, the check-ins had evolved into something else. It had become a friendship.

"Mr. Whiskers did something remarkable last night," Martinez said, settling onto Claire's couch with a cup of tea that tasted exactly like comfort. The tea always tasted exactly right in Claire's flat—one of the small improvements that came with living in proximity to a contented cosmic cat.

Official lady here for talking time. Good. Food lady likes talking time.

"Did he achieve enlightenment?" Claire asked, curling up in the armchair across from Martinez. "Open a portal to the dimension of cat treats? Finally learn to use the litter box consistently?"

"Better." Martinez's eyes were bright with amusement. "He fixed my shower."

"Your shower?"

"It's been running slightly cold for months. I kept meaning to call a plumber, but you know how it is—there's always another form to file, another incident to document, another prophetic hamster to check on." Martinez took a sip of her tea. "Last night, Mr. Whiskers sat in the bathroom for about an hour, purring at the pipes. Just... purring. Very intensely. Very focused. This morning, the water came out at exactly the right temperature. Perfect. First time in years."

Other cat makes pipes feel better. Smart cat.

Mungus, draped across Claire's lap like a particularly warm blanket, purred his approval.

"He's learning," Claire said. "Finding his own way to help."

"That's what I thought. He's not powerful like Mungus—Dr. Crumpet says he'll probably never develop full cosmic abilities. But he's figured out that he can make small improvements. The shower this week. Last month, he spent three days staring at my computer until it stopped making that grinding noise. The month before that, he somehow convinced the plant on my windowsill to stop dying."

Small improvements important. Every cosmic creature finds own path.

"You know what I appreciate most about this?" Claire said slowly. "Having someone who understands. My mum thinks I've lost my mind—she keeps sending me job listings for 'normal' careers. My old university friends stopped calling after I started talking about reality fluctuations at dinner parties. But you *get* it."

"I get it," Martinez agreed. "When I tried to explain Mr. Whiskers's shower intervention to my sister, she asked if I needed professional help. Not the plumbing kind—the psychological kind." She laughed, but there was old hurt in it. "But you—you'd just nod and make a note for the incident report."

"Form 52-F: Plumbing Improvements of Mysterious Origin."

"Harold's already drafted it. He was thrilled. Said it was the most creative application of the form he'd seen in decades."

They laughed together, and Claire felt something warm settle in her chest. She had spent so long being alone with her strange life—first as a graduate student nobody understood, drowning in research about civilizations that nobody thought mattered, then as the owner of a cosmic cat nobody believed in. Now she had a friend who understood completely. Who didn't need explanations. Who could sit in comfortable silence while their cats did impossible things in the background.

Good sounds. Food lady and official lady making happy sounds together. This is good friendship.

"Can I tell you something?" Martinez said quietly, setting down her tea. "Before all this—before the Ministry, before Mr. Whiskers started purring at my plumbing—I was thinking about quitting. The job, I mean. I'd been doing it for fifteen years, and I felt like I'd stopped making a difference. Just pushing papers, managing crises, never actually helping anyone."

"What changed?"

"You. Watching you fight for Mungus." Martinez met

Claire's eyes. "You were so fierce, so determined. You didn't care about protocols or procedures or proper channels. You just loved your cat and refused to let anyone take him away. It reminded me why I got into this work in the first place. Not for the paperwork—for the people. The families dealing with impossible situations. The beings who need someone to fight for them."

Claire felt tears prickling at her eyes. "I didn't know that."

"How could you? You were too busy being brave." Martinez smiled. "But watching you—it woke something up in me. Made me want to be brave too. So I stayed. And now I have a cat who fixes plumbing and a friend who understands, and I'm happier than I've been in years."

Official lady found purpose again. Good. All creatures need purpose.

"Same time next week?" Martinez asked, standing to leave.

"I'll have the kettle ready," Claire promised. "And maybe some of those biscuits Mungus keeps manifesting. The ones that taste like contentment."

"Those are genuinely unsettling. In a delicious way."

Biscuits appropriate. Will manifest more.

After Martinez left, Claire sat for a long moment with Mungus in her lap, thinking about friendship and purpose and the strange ways life could surprise you.

"You know what you did?" she said softly to him. "You didn't just save me. You helped save her too. And the Hartley family. And probably hundreds of other people who are living slightly better lives because you exist."

Obvious. Am very important cat. Have always said this.

"Yes," Claire agreed, laughing. "You've always said this."

Because is always true.

Outside, the stars were coming out, slightly brighter than usual—as if the universe was showing off, just a little, for the two of them.

Home

That evening, after Martinez left and Claire had filed the day's reports, she sat on her couch with Mungus in her lap and watched the sunset turn her windows into stained glass.

The aurora effects danced across her ceiling, gentle and beautiful. The coffee maker hummed contentedly in the kitchen, having learned exactly how she liked her evening tea. Outside, she could hear neighbors chatting in the street, their conversations carrying the warm, unhurried quality that had become normal in this part of London.

Good sounds. Good lights. Good lap. Good everything.

"I never told you this," Claire said softly, "but when they took you—when Harwick won that vote and they carried you away—I thought I'd lost everything. Not just you, but... everything I'd started to believe about myself. That I was strong enough to fight for what mattered. That I could be brave when it counted."

Remember dark time. Don't like remembering.

"But I was wrong. I hadn't lost anything. I just had to learn that being brave isn't about never being scared. It's about being scared and fighting anyway." She looked down at him. "You taught me that. Walking into that containment carrier to protect me—that was the bravest thing I've ever seen."

Would do again. Would always do for food lady.

"I know." She felt tears prickling at her eyes. "That's what makes it so remarkable. That you trusted me even when you were terrified. That you kept trusting me even after everything that happened."

Trust is. Just is. Like breathing.

Outside, the evening star appeared in the purpling sky. Claire watched it twinkle, thinking about all the impossible things that had become her ordinary life.

"You know what I realized?" she said. "I spent years studying civilizations that failed. That saw warnings and ignored them, that had chances to change and couldn't. I thought I was studying failure. But I wasn't."

Food lady making important sounds. Will listen.

"I was studying what happens when love isn't strong enough. When the connections between people aren't deep enough to overcome fear. Those civilizations didn't fail because they were stupid. They failed because they forgot how to trust each other."

She looked down at Mungus, who was gazing up at her with eyes that contained reflected starlight.

"We didn't fail. We trusted each other through impossible things. And that trust—that's what saved us. That's what saves anyone."

Good understanding. Food lady very wise now.

"I learned it from you."

Obviously. Am excellent teacher.

She laughed, and the sound seemed to make the aurora effects brighten. Outside, a shooting star traced a gentle arc across the sky—natural or cosmic, she couldn't tell anymore, and she'd stopped caring about the difference.

Perfect moment. Perfect night. Perfect food lady.

"Same time tomorrow?" Claire asked, as if it were a question.

Same time every day. Forever. This is arrangement.

She settled deeper into the couch, her cosmic cat purring in her lap, her strange and wonderful life humming along around her. Tomorrow there would be more forms to file, more incidents to assess, more impossible things to document. But tonight, there was just this: warmth, contentment, and the quiet certainty that she had found exactly where she was meant to be.

Through the window, London glittered with a thousand small lights—ordinary and extraordinary, natural and cosmic, all woven together into something that looked remarkably like hope.

Mungus shifted in Claire's lap, pressing his forehead against her chin. She felt his purr rumble through her, steady and whole, and outside, a single shooting star traced its arc across the darkening sky.

Good night, food lady.

"Good night, Mungus."

Neither of them moved.

Character List

MAIN CHARACTERS

Mungus
Seven-year-old cat. Simple philosophy: if it fits in his mouth, probably food. Adopted by Claire three years ago. Consumed the Seal of Final Things, achieving cosmic significance. Thinks in italicized observations about "food lady" and his environment.

Claire Pemberton
Graduate student in Applied Apocalyptics. Late twenties (implied). Has documented history of anxiety. Fiercely protective of Mungus. Thesis: studying civilizations that ignored warnings and destroyed themselves. Uses priceless artifacts as paperweights because her grant doesn't cover furniture.

Character List

ALLIES

Agent Martinez
Ministry of Defence: Special Projects and Irregular Situations Branch. Woman in her forties. Practical, warm beneath professional exterior. Has a cat named Mr. Whiskers (who she got at age eight). Becomes Claire's primary ally and friend.

Harold
Demon. Class C Manifestation of Mild Inconvenience. Size of a house cat, small filed-for-safety horns, decorative wings, expression of profound embarrassment. Originally summoned during a filing error. Loves bureaucracy with genuine passion. Appointed himself official note-taker. Types on a 1940s typewriter connected to modern systems.

Dr. Wilhelmina Crumpet
Woman in her sixties. Academic tenure achieved by proving impossible things are statistically inevitable. Wears temporal spectacles. Walking stick that buzzes. Has faced down bureaucratic stupidity many times before.

Professor Blackwood
Claire's academic advisor. Carries briefcase with supernatural detection equipment. Declared the Seal "moderately ominous but probably dormant." Thirty years

studying theoretical manifestations—emotional when theory becomes practice.

Dr. Elena Ramirez
Veterinarian specializing in supernatural creatures. Woman in her fifties. Calm competence. Works from a clinic that looks like veterinary science crossed with alchemy. Has a small dragon napping in a cat bed. Fifteen years ago, lost a gryphon's bond through unnecessary surgery—now advocates fiercely for natural approaches.

ANTAGONISTS

Gerald Harwick
Assistant Deputy Under-Secretary for Fiscal Oversight and Resource Allocation. Thin, severe-looking. Views kindness as a budget line item to be eliminated. Prepared, organized, strategic. Attacks people to discredit arguments. Used same tactics in "the Sullivan case" (2008) and "Morrison incident" (three years later)—both entities permanently contained.

Directeur Beaumont
French Ministry of Impossible Affairs. Severe woman. Allies with Harwick on cost concerns and surgical intervention. Her feed keeps inserting "meow" when she speaks dismissively about Mungus.

COMMITTEE MEMBERS

Deputy Minister Warren
(Reality Maintenance) Tired, weary, wants to be elsewhere. Votes yes reluctantly.

Davidson
Home Office representative. Pinch-faced. Had already decided before the meeting. Votes yes.

Unnamed woman
Health and Safety Executive. Hesitates, shows sympathy, but follows Harwick. Votes yes.

Unnamed man
Housing representative. Won't make eye contact. Votes yes. Later runs from the room clutching documents "like a shield against guilt."

Peters
Foreign Office junior liaison. Youngest member, under thirty. Looks sick about it but votes yes.

Thompson
DEFRA representative. Round-faced. Watches Mungus with genuine interest. Votes no (slowly, deliberately, defiantly).

MINOR/MENTIONED

David Dawson
Technician Grade 2, monitoring station beneath Whitehall. First to detect the anomaly. "I think we have an unscheduled cat."

Mr. Whiskers
Agent Martinez's cat. Practicing cosmic purring. Created a glowing mushroom from a dead ficus.

Two technicians in grey jumpsuits
Carry the containment carrier. Tired voices. Have done this before.

About the Author

Kysa Steele is an IT professional by day, and by night an author, TTRPG GM, cat servant, and wife (though the order depends on which cat is asking). She grew up devouring books and plotting to write her own. While newly minted as an indie author, she's been telling elaborate, occasionally cursed stories at the TTRPG table for years.

Her cat-centric fiction spans dark fantasy, detective noir, portal adventures, and apocalyptic comedy. The Infurnal Catastrophe series features a cursed demon princess and infernal magic, while the Orange Protocol follows a hard-boiled detective trapped in a cat's body and scattered across a psychic network of orange tabbies. Her Unfamiliar Territory series stars Mischief, a portal-hopping cat whose curiosity threatens entire dimensions. She spends her time building worlds and trying to unravel her cats' many conspiracies.

She lives in Texas with her husband and a cadre of furry overlords. Nori and Mochi are the latest recruits, while Nox, nicknamed the Demon Princess, claimed dominion during the writing of Curse Meow Not. Jake Speed and his sister Ripley occupy the middle ranks, and the eldest, Cid, remains her watchful shadow and self-appointed bodyguard.

Also by Kysa Steele

Curse Meow Not

Velzara was forged for the apocalypse—destined to burn worlds. Now she's a fluffy black housecat adopted by a young witch who thinks "Nox" is just a stray with attitude problems. But when ancient curses start rearranging the walls and something far more dangerous than a fallen demon princess is lurking in the house, Velzara faces an impossible choice: reclaim her monstrous birthright or protect the mortal girl who's starting to feel like home.

Containment Not Recommended

Luis Cannon was a hardboiled detective until the Cognichonk shattered his consciousness across a psychic network of orange cats. When they sync, they solve mysteries with noir narration. When the signal fades, they scream at ceiling fans. But something's wrong—cats are going lucid, occult sigils are spreading like magical malware, and the Cognichonk is choosing sides.

Cat Out of Luck

Mischief just wanted to jazz up a boring ritual, nap, and maybe snag a few sardines for later. Instead, he got trapped in a human body and discovered something is hunting familiars across dimensions, harvesting them as magical batteries. The universe made a terrible mistake giving him any responsibility. He's going to make it everyone's problem.

The Twelve Days of Catmas

Krampus has spent three hundred years alone in his lair, filing suffering reports and telling himself he's fine. Then a small black cat shows up and refuses to leave. Each day brings new chaos—argumentative partridges, therapy doves, unionizing hens, explosive geese. What Krampus doesn't know is that Yule isn't just a cat. He's the Spirit of Festive Misrule, and every disaster is surgical precision designed to crack through centuries of isolation. Therapy has never been this catastrophic. Or this purr-suasive.

Nine Lives, Zero Paperwork

Brentley didn't mean to become a cosmic fugitive. He just wanted a ride. But when an orange tabby with reality-warping powers and a pathological lying problem hijacks cargo hauler Jarik Venn's ship, things spiral fast. The Familiar Reclamation Bureau—a hyper-bureaucratic agency staffed by disgruntled former familiars—wants Brentley back. Brentley wants to be worshipped as the god-king he clearly is. Jarik just wants his ship to stop being on fire. Between hairballs that violate physics and a cat who takes credit for every accident, this might be the worst day of Jarik's life. Or the start of something he'll never escape.

Want more cats and chaos?

Join my Patreon for weekly chapter drops, exclusive stories, world-building lore, and behind-the-scenes chaos at patreon.com/kysasteele

Enjoyed this book?

Reviews help other readers find these stories! If you have a moment, leaving a review on Amazon, Goodreads, or your retailer of choice means the world to indie authors like me.

Want a free short story?

Sign up for my newsletter and get 2 short stories from my other series. **kysasteele.com/newsletter**

www.ingramcontent.com/pod-product-compliance
Lightning Source LLC
LaVergne TN
LVHW041708060526
838201LV00043B/628